AF444441

Cristina Tata

It's a life I dream

of loving you

"It is not in the stars to hold our destiny but in ourselves."

William Shakespeare

Prologue

"How the hell did I get to this point?"

I ask myself like every morning, looking my eyes reflected in the mirror. They are tired eyes, marked by an evident bluish halo. Eyes that do not find the true rest for weeks. Since months already I am like a prisoner of myself, a self that I do not recognize and that I hate, but that come back on time every morning, knocking at my door insistently.

I do not understand how it is possible to be precipitated in a situation like this, like in a chasm from which it is impossible to go back. It seems crazy to me that in such a short time my life has changed so much, and I always wonder where she ended up, the other me, the one who would fight and that it would have come out of this state of torpor like a hibernation.

There are days when I want nothing more than to sleep.

Sleep seems to have become the only one cure and the only trusted friend, since only by sleeping can I not think. But it is a restless sleep, which in the morning leaves me even more tired and free of forces from the previous evening.

By now I believe I look more and more like a

larva enclosed in its cocoon, inside which it prefers to remain in hiding, rather than go out and unfold its wings. So I remain motionless in my physical and mental torpor, to bask in my own sadness and my unhappiness.

What a terrible desolation and disappointment of myself!

I well know that I should react and stop crying myself out, but I can not and I do not want to do it; pessimism has taken over and crying is my only relief valve. I can not restrain myself from doing it. I have nothing else to cling to, no more than to let me go adrift...

1

I am Rebecca, and 2 weeks ago I have been fired.

I received the well-served after years of sacrifices and complete dedication to my work, and I do not know if more this to make me feel bad or the sentence pronounced by the right arm of the boss, used to fire me.

"I am so sorry Rebbi" Viola said, "but you know with this crisies also us, as you can easily understand, we were forced to make some cuts. And you unfortunately with that series of mistakes..." She made a pause, like to give me the time to metalobolize what she just comminicated to me. "However you are a smart girl, with an eccellent curriculum, and you'll see that you will not have a hard time finding another job", she tried to sugarcoat it.

Staff reduction, crisis, errors... hell not! That bastard of my boss, actually former boss by now, wanted to make me pay, holding onto my mistakes made during the last work done for the couple Alghise.

I admit I was a little risky in not wanting to follow the instructions given to me about the apartment to be restored, therefore making them completely out of their mind and taking almost the risk of a complaint. Usually I am very professional and I try to satisfy all the needs of the customer, but there is a limit to everything. I cannot certantly go against my aesthetic sense! Their requests were devoid of any logic, besides being a real affront to all the canons of harmony, balance and beauty.

I know, the situation probably got a little out of my hands, especially because of a temporary period of stress due to the cancellation of my imminent marriage. But I remain sure of the fact that this was just a trivial excuse. The truth is that Paolo has never digested my refusal towards him.

Since Giulio dumped me infact, in less than a month from our wedding, he did not stop to hover over me.

I suspected that he was hitting on me since a long time before, until these suspicions have turned into reality. But despite my despair of this period, a subject like him I could never ever take it into consideration, even if I had been abstinent for years!

Rather chastity for life!

I hated his inability to roll his "r" and the way he pronounced my name, rolling the first letter on his tongue. I always thought he was a treacherous and slimy person, as it turned out to be. I already hated him as a boss, and the only thought of being touched and kissed by him makes me cringe to say the least.

Obviously, losing my job from one day to the next

was certainly not part of my plans for the future, and especially not after having suffered another very hard blow just a few months ago.

And so here I come to a dead end of my life, where I really do not know what else to expect.

Some mornings I get up from the bed that I looked like a zombie and I wandered home in my pajamas for the rest of the time. It seems to me it does not make sense to even dress me.

Honey, my dwarf bunny, follows me undeterred in every rooms. He looks at me as if I were a strange creature, then he comes close to me, smells me and gives me a lick. In the end, when he decided it was always me, he cuddled on the kitchen's mat to take a nap. He seems to be the only one who still recognizes the same person in me, and to take care of him, is distracting me from my many thoughts.

I brush his soft and silky hair as if it was a ritual, caressing his face, a gesture that he seems to appreciate very much, remaining still and squinting his hazel eyes. Contact with what seems to be a snowball is comforting and indispensable for me.

I put some straw in his bowl and immediately he happily paws to get his usual daily feast.

Sometimes I wish I could be in his place! No thought, no worries, just cuddles and lots of food...

2

One of the rare times when I can really distract myself and do not think about anything is when I'm with Andrea, my best friend ever, as well as my roommate.

After weeks of lethargy, this morning he convinced me to go out.

In reality it is a real imposition, since with Andrea there is no discussion, and today he has planned to go shopping, although know perfectly well how much I hate shopping's centers, especially on weekends.

Confusion, queues in stores, but above all - people and more people!

The overflowing places of people have never been for me. On the contrary, the more I can be alone, the better it is for my nerves that go absolutely in escalation in the crowd, so much so that sometimes I think of looking like demophobia!

But Andrea, alas, is the classic shopping addict and for my bad luck I can not deny anything to him. So I find myself having to get up at a time now unthinkable for me in recent weeks, like seven thirty in the morning, and to dress. I wear my usual worned out jeans and a too dated shirt and I'm ready.

I did not really care about dressing trendy, on the contrary, I always tried to have my own personal style, without ever following the trends of the moment. So much so that the idea of being equal to the mass causes me a certain annoyance, from which I prefer to distinguish myself above all in this moment, in which even the thought of having to taking off my pajamas makes me uncomfortable.

I go to the mirror, I quickly fix my hair and put a little pencil on my eyes and a touch of blush on the cheekbones, just enough to not make me look like a corpse.

I put on my sneakers and I close the door behind me, feeling in no way ready for the *tour de force* of which I will soon be the victim.

Andrea, always early-riser as far as I am concern, is already outside waiting for me.

As soon as he sees me he gives me a lightning glance, but long enough to pass me to X-rays.

"My dear, you immediately need some restyling!" he tells, while I read in his face a total disapproval for my appearance.

"I do not need it. I look very good." I deny. "In anycase I am not a car!" I say jocking, climbing on his Smart yellow bird's color. This car fully reflects the character and liveliness of the person sitting next to me. Sometimes I envy him, and I would love to be like him. Although his has never been an easy life, Andrea has always managed to overcome the difficulties, not caring about the whole world. Having to confess his homosexuality, face the judgment and the ignorance of the people and of his own family, who never understood or even less supported him, was certainly not a small thing for him. Despite all this, however, the release of the enormous weight he had to carry it for years made it reborn to new life.

In this disastrous period of my existence, I wish I could have the chance to start everything from scratch again. Undoubtedly it would be great! Being able to go through all the stages one by one, but without making the mistakes that have cost me sufference and problems. It would be easy, maybe even too much. But this is the real life, and in one way or another I have to be able to face it and get it back.

But not today...

Andrea starts the car, unaware of my thoughts, and of the notes of my favorite song we begin to hover in the cockpit.

We're caught in a trap
I can't walk out
Because I love you too much baby..., we both sing loudly, thing that manages to make me feel better right away.

I started listening to The King when I was still in middle school, and since then I have never stopped. Once on the radio they had transmitted a song of his (I do not remember well which one it was), but when I heard that deep voice and at the same indefinable time, I had been completely in bliss. The next day I had recovered an old vinyl in my father's record collection (of which up to that point I didn't even know of its existance), and I think I literally consumed it by dint of listening to it.

If I think of the high school years, and to how much I have been made fun of for my passion by my classmates, I still have to smile.

All girls, without exception, in those days they were listening to new emerging groups composed of beardless, probably with as much talent as facial hair. They literally tore their hair for what I liked to call with the nickname of "bambocci". Instead I, that I could never even attend a concert of my idol, their attitude I did not conceive it, and I was e was satisfied to have the room invaded by posters stuck everywhere. There was not one corner of my romm where there was not one of his picture, or some excerpt of his songs, or some drawing that represented him. Not to mention the countless CDs, videotapes, vinyl and books. I had learn by hearth all his repertoire and everything about his private life.

And so everyone saw me as the strange one, who

liked to listen to music from "the Advent Christ", as they called it, a dead guy buried for years.

In all honesty, I have never cared a damn about their criticism, on the contrary, in my turn I was enjoing very much making fun of them on the fact that were amusing those caracthers that were for me insignificant. I thought they would listen to their songs just because they were fashionable at the, because as for my view point, from there to some years nobody would ever remember them.

Some years later, in a music shop, thank to this passion of mine, I came to know Andrea. Both of us that afternoon we put our eyes on one Cd, both of us bewildered about the fact that were still missing compilations from our respectives collections.

After looking at each other for at least five minutes and having an animated discussion on who of the two had first seen the object of our contention, we started to chit chat, almost making a competition of who of us knew more song titles than the other and of the dates of the pubblications, until we found ourselves drinking a capuccino in a cafe'. So as this morning, at distance of many years...

3

Find a parking slot in a shopping center on Sunday is a real struggle for survival fight!

Obviously I have no doubt that Andra bought his car, more like a box than a car, just to be able to sneak in the narrowest space of the super croweded parking lots.

He loves these kind of things, I definitely NOT!

However now I find myself in this infernal place, even if I already regret my confortable bad, that to avoid to think too much about it, I taste the hot chocolate croissant soaked in the coffe. Basically now I depend on caffeine, despite I hated it until sometime ago. In this period instead I could not live without it, and I feel the need especially now, if I think that soon I will be literally dragged from one shop to another until exhaustation.

Andrea will never step out of this place until he will has visisted them all, and I feel already terribly tired by only thinking about it.

"Come on, stop making that face. It looks like you are about to face a firing squad!" he said to be smilying, already looking forward for the pleasure of his imminent purchases.

"Which face? That of a poor girl forced to wake up at an inhumane schedule to be dragged in a place completely hostile for her?" prompltly replied.

"Since when seven in the morning would be considered an inhumane time?", he glares at me. "Come on, how you make it tragic. Instead let's harry up. You'll see that you will not regret it."

I already regret it!

I wonder why he ever let me convince.

We leave the first store already overloaded with bags of various sizes and this is just the beginning!

Following that we enter a shoes shop, where obviously he can not avoid to buy 2 pair: of black mocassins (something that a men with style should never give upf!), and sneakers of a known brand, which assures me one day he will need them, since he has every intention of starting to jog!

I pretend to believe it only to please him.

Andrea certantly has never been a lover of movement. Except when it comes to shopping, of course! In those cases it then turns into a giant slalom champion, obstacle race and marathon runner, in one shot.

His only fortune is that although he has never

practiced any sport in his life, he has always had a dry body and really nothing bad for a sedentary guy like him.

Then it's the turn of the perfumery, and then again of a bag shop where he buys a trolley, missing from his maniacal's bag collection.

Now I'm exhausted and on the verge of a nervous breakdown.

"Andrea, please!" I say exhausted, "I have a urgent need to make a stop at the toilet and to feed me!", I look at him pleadingly.

"Ok, okay, you whiner!" he makes me grimace. "Somctimes I wonder what I must have ever done wrong in a previous life to deserve you as a best friend!" His tone is joking, but I fulminated him instantly.

Our friendship has always been like this and I love it for this too. Andy is frank, and always says what he thinks without any, while risking to be too sincere sometimes. But as they say: *"Better a hard truth than a sweet lie..."*

We sit at the tables of one of the many clubs, already full of hungry people who can not wait to stuff themselves with food - just like me - and I order a pizza with vegetables and peach tea.

"At least this will not make me fat!" I say while filling my glass, and already feeling guilt takes possession of me.

"You always have a physical envy, and you know it", Andrea replies. "If only you tried to put it a little more on show…" In his voice I perceive the usual tone of reprimand.

"You know very well how I think about it", I replied. "Displaying merchandise is not from me. And then I'm not at all fit as you say", and in fact lately I feel more and more uncomfortable with myself. "You do not have to lie to please me. Admit it, I'm not so much desirable anymore!" I exclaim with dismay.

"If you do not feel fit as you say, why do not you do something?" he askes.

Here we go again! Another time!

Now he will give me yet another lecture.

"In the morning you could very well get up early and go running. Infact, what would you say if we go together next week?"

"Will see…" for nothing convinced I replied to that.

"So Rebecca! Do you wnat to give yourself a joilt? You are sliding your life into your hands." Suddenly his voice become more severe, and catching me off guard almost makes me jump from the chair. "You can not go on like this. Take back what you deserve!" insists.

"It is easy for you to talk. You did not have to bear all what I have been in the last few months."

"You say?"

Of course, sometimes I really act like one perfect bitch!

I should not be so sour with him. Andrea always helped and supported me, but unfortunately my self-defence mechanism shoots up more often authomatically, without me being able to control it.

"Ok then, just keep basking in your unhappiness and thinking about what you do not have anymore. Why it is not just about the right job? You still think of Giulio!" Say these last words in an overly direct way.

"What does Giulio have to do with it now?" I ask altered. "It's been four months now since he left me. I do not think of him for quite a while anymore." chin, also and above all to myself.

My ex boy-friend is a wound that often burns, and a lot.

The story with him still torments me. Too important to be able to forget it so quickly, I never really committed myself so that I could erase it completely. In fact I have not yet gone out with anyone else, just to name one!

It seems obvious to me at this point that the decision to remain holed up in my shell and not wanting to leave for any reason, is in no way revocable, not in the near future at least.

"Why you always have to bring up Giulio? You know that I prefer not to talk about it", I rebuke him.

"Okay. I'm sorry. But I can no longer see you in this state. I love you too much to allow you to give up living!"

"I know, and I thank you for this. But you do not have to worry, I can take care of myself. And then with you close I have no way out!" I smile at him putting an end to this unhappy subject for me.

We eat chatting about this and that. Suddenly, however, I realize that I have completely lost his attention, which has instead focused on the table next to ours, to which he is sitting a guy looking elegant and to which Andrea is launching unequivocal signs of priming.

I start kicking his shins under the table, but he ignores me completely, continuing to flirt with his sight ith that guy. At this point, no longer knowing where to hide the face, I get up with the excuse of going to pay the bill.

Time to queue and pay for our lunch, which I find Andrea sitting at the table of the stranger.

I can not believe! I could not leave this Casanova alone even for a moment!

I think I have no choice but to intrude on their conversation.

"Very pleased I am Rebecca, a dear friend of Andrea" I say holding out my hand that he tightens with decision.

"The pleasure is all mine. My name is Marco."

His tone is so seductive that if he had not already pointed my best friend, I could even fall at his feet.

"Rebbi sit here with us" Andrea invites me. "Marco was telling me what brought him to Pavia. Just think, he just moved here from Palermo. Is not it a crazy coincidence that he too comes from our wonderful Sicily?" enthusiastic question.

Wow! All this information exchange in less than five minutes? To say the least!

"So you moved to work? Or was it some other reason to bring you here?" I ask inquiringly, looking with this question of understand if there is another him or maybe another her, or even both. You never know today!

I do not to show to be rude, but Andrea's latest love affairs inevitably lead me to be prevented against anyone.

Andy has always been the so-called magnet for desperate cases. He meets almost one a month and then I find him in the kitchen to eat tons of chocolate, his only way to dilute the amorous disappointments.

Anyway, this guy is undoubtedly a beautiful boy. Moro, deep eyes and intense gaze, tall and with a good body, olivorous complexion and a fascinating southern accent. We can certainly not deny that Andrea did not take a delicious morsel on the hook! I am attracted to it myself. Too bad it seems to have no eyes except for my friend, who already seems to hang from his lips.

It's done!

Before saying goodbye, our new knowledge gives Andrea his business card, adding a *call* between my lips. In passing I can read written *Marco Poggi, lawyer*.

Who knows why I had already guessed it.

The same profession of Andy, who, however, in the last period has decided to deal mainly with pro-bono cases, dedicating himself to the most needy cases, not able to face the costs associated with professional advice. A praiseworthy activity and for him very rewarding, which absolutely does not use as a personal showcase, but only to help others, for a question that he defines as well as ethics and morality, even and above all duty.

This is one of the many reasons that push me to esteem him not only as a man, but also as a professional, and to feel grateful to have a person like him beside me.

4

We finally return home when is already very late.
Thank God this day has came to an end.

I throw myself on the couch, I turn on the TV and a start running the channels, but as usual there are only programs that do not capture my interest.

I do not have time to relax, however, that my phone starts ringing.

I look at the display and read *Mom*.

Oh no! I absolutely do not want to talk to her at this moment!

Surely it will end up making me the same sermons of all time and I'm tired of hearing them repeat it. So I let the phone keep ringing. But it is insistent, and at the third call I get convinced to answer.

"Hi darling", I hear at the other end of the phone.

"Hi mom" I answer with a bored voice.

"Why do you never answer? I'll call you at least ten times!"

Exagerated, like all the times.

"I started to worry."

"Don't worry mom, I'm fine" I try to reassure her. I am sorry that you are worried because of me, but being evasive has now become the watchword when I talk to her. I should be like this, to avoid a storm of questions and reprimand that punctually were falling on me and that I can not longer bear.

"Are you sure you are doing fine? I don't like this voice at all" she sights, now clearly resigned to have a complete a disaster as a daughter.

"Sure. You do not have to worry" I garantee, and after a few minutes I close the conversation with the usual reccomendations and the usual ones *I love each other*.

Suddently I feel tired and sleepy, therefore I decide to go to bed early. Tomorrow I will have to face a job interview, and it will certainly be better if I get well rested and without bags under my eyes!

This is a position like a visual merchandiser in a downtown boutique, role with which I don't have any relevancy, even if in the past I was a shoop assistant to pay off my designer'study. However arrived at this point I prefer to try all the possible ways, without foreclosing any.

Passion, creativity, strong aesthetic sense,

curiosity, are all qualities that certainly do not miss me; therefore I think that I can be suitable to play a role like this, at least until I have found something more akin to me and my work so far.

It is not at all easy to find a job these days, despite a degree and an excellent track record behind, and I would not have believed it so complicated if I had not found myself in this situation. On the contrary, I was convinced that the bad news about the crisis and the lack of jobs that are constantly heard on TV and are read in the newspapers, were only conjectures designed to create the usual false alarmism. Instead, for some aspects, I had to change my mind.

When a few weeks ago I had to take a good "kick in the back" from the studio from where I was working, I felt literally losted. That place had been my second home for several years, especially after my break with Giulio. I devoted myself to my work, body and soul, both because it is my passion, but also and mainly because in this way there was not much time left to think about my absolutely disastrous sentimental situation.

Giulio had almost managed to ruin my life, demolishing a good part of confidence and security on myself that I had built up over the years.

As a child, and as a teenager, I was very shy and introverted. The most joyful and carefree part of me

I could express it only in my family and with my very few friends, that in reality we always could them only in one hand, of which moreover was always missing some fingers!

During the years of my school career I have never been the girl who showed off, the most popular in the class, the one around which everything going, from parties, trips or performances. I was the nerd. The one to which everyone turned to get their homework on the first day of school when they returned from vacation, and from which to copy during the checks.

Ever since then, many things could be understood about what my future life would be like. Unexpectedly, however, the last year of high school I had undergone a change, not only interior, but also aesthetic. I was now largely tired of being treated like an ugly duckling, and I had decided that it was finally time to turn into a swan and show everyone what I was. Enough with insecurities, enough glasses half a centimeter thick, just dressing and behaving in a clumsy way, but above all enough shyness.

That was precisely the year when I had made friends with Andrea, who undoubtedly had managed to give me a considerable boost in my change, so that in the end I myself had difficulty to recognize me.

But suddenly, after so many years, she has

reappeared again, coming back stronger than ever, or maybe it's just me who is not enough anymore...

5

The alarm is ringing and I don't have any intention to get up, but I have to do it because in a couple of hours I'll have to show up for the interview.

So I get up from the bed, as always reluctantly, I go to the bathroom and refresh my face. I look in the mirror, and what I see reflected is a real disaster!

Thus begins my odyssey.

I do not know what to wear, since by now dressing up has almost become an option for me; so

I rush to ask Andy for help, which of course at this time of the morning is already washed shaved and dressed, and is already drinking his first coffee of the day!

"Well risen sleepy" greet me.

"Good Morning" I say, placing a kiss in his cheek. "This morning I have that interview with you I had mentioned... But look at me: I look like a zombie just come out of a rave party!"

"Don't worry, I'll take care of it."

"Thank you. Because I was almost thinking about going out in pigiama!" I esclaim.

"From you I expect this and more!" he replies.

"You know I'm a desperate case, and you're my only hero. What I would do without you?" I say hugging him.

"I really do not know" he admits. "Come on, let's hurry up. Time is running out, and I have to transform you from a mass that is shapeless to something vaguely resembles a woman!"

"Ehi!" I say, pulling the towel in his face. "Do not exagerate!"

Andrea laughs, and immediately gets to work.

Go to the bathroom and fill up the bath with steaming water and fragrant salts, that within a few minutes invade the house with an intense smell of sandalwood and vanilla. Then he begins to pull out from the beautycase a whole series of objects almost completely forgotten to me.

I smile, imagining him as a sort of Mary Poppins from whose bag he can extract anything. But this thought immediately makes me regret asking him for help, because I know very well that he will subject me to a whole series of tortures - starting with waxing! - that I do not really think I can handle.

I must however admit that the hot bath is absolutely regenerating, and I let myself go immersed in the foam to the tip of my nose, trying to clear my mind from the thoughts that crowd it.

Luckily for me it works.

I leave the tub in a good mood, and of this I just have to thank my irreplaceable ally in the fight against the other me: the one who lets himself go, who feels defeated and who always sees the glass half empty.

"Thank you Andy. Without you I will be lost." And it is the pure and simple truth.

"Wait to thank me darling. Do it after I have put you under pressure!"

Why does this phrase almost sound like a threat to my ears?

"So, you think to ear that Marco again?" I am asking this mainly to not think about what is waiting me.

"Actually, last night, after you went to sleep, he called me back, and after five minutes of conversation he invited me to drink something from him...", he says maliciously.

"I can not believe it! I can not just leave you alone! And how was the evening?"

From his look I understand very well everything down to the smallest details.

"Ok, I do not want to know anything else. Pretend you did not ask for it!" I pretend embarrassment, even if in reality the joy I see reflected in his eyes can only make me happy.

After more than an hour of torment, at the end I leave the house radiant.

It had been a long time since I took so much care of my appearance or allowed someone else to do it for me, and Andy has been absolutely wonderful, as he only knows how to be.

I still have some time, so I walk towards the boutique without excessive haste, and after a few minutes I'm already in front of the windows.

I'm in advance, as always, a manic of punctuality as I am, so I take this opportunity to have a look here and there at the new arrivals in autumn.

Suddenly I look at the time and I realize that only two minutes are left at eleven o'clock, so I approach a saleswoman intent on helping a client. *Maria*, I read on the card that is hunging on her shirt. From the aspect, cared down to the smallest detail, seems to be slightly younger than me.

Thank God Andrea has polished me, otherwise I

would have had no chance at this place already!

I wait for Maria to finish speaking and introduce myself. "Good Morning. I am Rebecca. I have a interview at eleven with Mrs De Marchi."

"Yes, sure. The manager is waiting for her" tells me. "Please take a seat upstairs. First door to the right."

"Thanks" I reply courteously.

As I climb the steps I start to be assaulted by anxiety and I wonder if it was a good idea to introduce myself here this morning.

I'm not cut for this job. Precisely that I understand less than zero about fashion and new trends!

Fortunately, the interview does not last long, after twenty minutes, an *"I will let her know"* and a handshake, I find myself already on the way back, I already find myself on the way back.

I wonder what it took to spend almost two hours to get back in for a few minutes. What an absolute waste of time and energy!

The first thing Mrs. De Marchi had asked me was to describe me with three adjectives. A real undertaking for me that I can never give me the right value.

Dynamic, I had answered first of all. But I had almost smiled when I said this word, since currently the maximum expression of this term that represents me is the obstacle course between the supermarket departments!

Creative. If by creativity we mean: "Which cake could I invent for the next weekend?", surely they are still. In fact it seems that in recent weeks churning out cakes and biscuits has become my only specialty. And the rest is the only thing that can distract me from my depression and my daily routine.

Suitable for working in a team. Another smile. Now the only team that I can be part of is the one formed by me, my rabbit and Andrea!

I decided to call this last one to confort me. I feel very down and I hope he can cheer me up.

Fortunately it is available and after a few rings answers the phone.

"Hi darling. So, how did it go?" he askes me right away.

"Well..."

"What is wrong with Rebbi?" question worried, since from my tone of voice will have already guessed my more than obvious disquiet.

"You really want to know? Is that I am really tired. Really very, very tired" I reply. "I can not understand why my life is falling apart. I feel like a broken vase of which no one, including me, can no longer put the pieces together again."

"You should not be so negative. You should have a bit of patience."

"I am sick and tired to have patience Andy!" I

scream without even realizing it.

"And then do something more concret to change this situation!"

"And what I should do in your opinion?"

I am really starting to get nervous.

"You might think about starting a studio of your own, just to name one. I told you more than once. You were anyway wasted in that company, and you know it very well."

"Are you kidding? Because if it were, you're not funny at all."

Is probably gone mad?

"In your opinion how could I do it? Be realist once and a while! I need a job, not other problems!"

"I am always real Rebecca, and I do not understand what's so absurd about my idea. I was in you I would think about it seriously. You need a real change in your life, and this could be the right way."

"I really don't think Andrea" I short cut. "See you at home." For me the question is definitely closed.

I conclude the phone call even more afflicted and nervous than before.

But what came in his mind?

I've always been very good at my job, undoubtedly very competent and with so much experience behind, but this certainly could not be sufficient.

For example, to begin with, where would I find

the money needed to start my own business?

Of course I can always turn to my parents, who certantly would not deny me their help, but I don't have any intention. And anyway at this moment I would not even have the strenght, neither the courage.

All of this is absolutely insane, and not just for an economic question. How could I stay afloat in a continuously falling market, and compete with such a ruthless competition?

Do not talk about it! I would never threw myself in such madness.

Of course I still have some savings in my account, even if a considerable part of what I managed to put aside in recent years has gone up in smoke for the organization of my marriage. When everything went off in the last moment, many expenses had already been dealt with and it was no longer possible to recover the money in advance. The deposit for the restaurant for example, as well as the advance for our honeymoon, had been completely lost. And then the invitations, the wedding favors, my wedding dress... That I kept in a box in my parents'house. At the mere memory I am still pervaded by a feeling of rage and discouragement. Wearing the white dress was my dream since childhood.

And then the wedding preparations had now came to an end, so much so that if only I closed my eyes I could already hear the notes of the wedding march playing for us. Instead everything went wrong, and if what happened and if what happened had not happened to me, I would probably have felt like the appearance of the usual film, in which the bride is planted on the altar.

Maybe I would have laughed too thinking about that poor woman who had remained there alone, with her bouquet of white roses in her hand, surrounded by a mass of guests - at least a hundred! - who looked at her incredulously, while someone among them left to run after the groom, who in the meantime had already given her up!

But all of this really happened, and I can not find anything funny nor droll, because is not an American Comedy, but the harsh reality of my life.

I wanted a fairytale wedding, but my story with Giulio taught me that fairy tales are just such and that the prince does not exist, not for me at least.

After ten years of engagement, it seems obvious to me that I can not cancel everything from one day to the next, just as Andrea would like, as if it were only a minor story.

I often still think back to what happened the last time I saw Giulio, the night when the world suddenly collapsed on me, and everything became meaningless to me. But even now, after some time, I can not give it a proper explanation...

6

I prepared for Giulio his favorite dish.

I like very much to cook, and it's a great way for me to be able to relax, even if I have never been able to dedicate the right time to this activity; because it is always taken from study or from work; but when I can, I love stay on the stoves.

It is all ready. Table settled, lightened candel, the pie that bakes in the oven and a delicious aroma that invades the house.

I put on makeup and worn skirt and heels - not too tall! -, something that normally is not my habit to do, except on very rare occasions.

This morning Giulio seemed strange to me, while he anticipated to have something important to tell me. I really do not know what it is and therefore I die of curiosity, but there is likely some change in view in work. He has always been an ambitious boy, much more than me.

Giulio and I graduated a few months apart from each other, and his career as an architect started right away in the family studio.

In fact, at the beginning he had insisted so much that I followed him, in fact his father would have taken me too as a trainee. I did not like the idea of working every day in close contact and having to depend on his family; so I immediately set out to find a job with my own strength, and I was immediately rewarded.

When Giulio returns home I can not help but notice his dark face.

I went to meet him, throwing his arms around his neck and welcoming him with a sparkling smile.

"Welcome back love" I tell him kissing him in his lips. "I have a surprise for you!" exclaimed enthusiastically, hoping to be able to change his mood.

"Hi Rebecca", he answers me in a very serious tone.

An alarm bell rings immediately in my head. Giulio calls me with my first name very rarely, generally only when he is nervous or angry, which does not happen often given his affable character.

"Something wrong?" I asked worried.

"I have to talk to you Rebbi."

"Well, we can always do it while we have dinner" I say, I say, trying to dampen the tension that has already been created between us.

"I think is better to do it now." His expression is more and more toughful.

"Agree." My voice is trembling.

"Come here. Seat down" he says pointing at the sofa'.

Another ugly sign.

In this moment I would like to not be here. I don't know why but I perceive a negative feeling, and I fear that this sensation in a fraction of a second can become a very harsh reality.

"I don't know from where to start" admits escaping my eyes.

Why he does not look in my eyes?

"I would try from the beginning" I say in a falsely

ironic tone, to try to keep my nerves calm.

"See Rebbi, for me it is not easy to find the right words..."

"Giulio please! Can we know what's happening?" I am more and more terrified by what I fear to hear.

"I am sorry. Making you suffer is the last thing I would like."

"Making me suffer? What does it means?" Actually I think I have already guessed everything, even if my mind still pretends not to understand.

I do not want to hear anymore!

"Rebecca, I think I am not longer in love with you. Not as it was once, and not as you are of me" he confesses all in one breath. "I do not know if the feeling I feel at this moment is enough, do you understand? You deserve better."

"No I don't understand!" I wish I could scream, but I can not. Not one sound comes out of my mouth.

"Rebbi, tell me something. Please. I believe that you too have noticed that things have changed for some time. This marriage would be a mistake. I'm sorry."

"You're sorry? You're just a damn son of a bitch!" I can finally scream at him. "What does it mean to say you're sorry? So why are you leaving me? Is there another woman? Tell me! I have the right to know it."

He is silent.

"Fuck answer me Giulio! Is there or not another

woman?" I weep at his chest and start beating him and crying at the same time.

"Cool down. And anyway certain words are not suit you, you know."

"Do not allow yourself to scold me. I speak like hell, I think! You have no rights over me."

"You are right. I'm so sorry. Anyway, no, there's no one else. I could never have done you like that."

"Ah no?" I pronounce almost laughing. "Why do you think that what you're doing to me is not destroying me anyway?"

"You will take Rebecca back when you understand that this is the right thing. We would both suffer, we would be unhappy, and this would make no sense."

"Nothing more makes sense to me right now. You're leaving me, just a few weeks from our marriage. Why are you doing this to me Giulio? I love you." I announce this phrase as if it were my last hope.

Perhaps he will change his mind, perhaps he will still want to marry me and spend the rest of his life with me.

"Tell me what I have to do Giulio. Please tell me. I still want to be your wife."

"There is nothing you can do Rebbi. It's not your fault, I want that this is very clear to you. It's just me. It's only my fault. I can not think of binding myself to you forever."

"Why now? Why not some months ago, when we took this decision? I can not understand. I can not believe this is really happening. Tell me it's just a stupid joke."

I feel now a prey of utter despair.

"I wish I could do it, believe me. I would like to find the right words, but there is no right explanation. Whatever I told you right now would not suffice to cushion the blow. Forgive me, if you can", saying this extends a hand to caress my face.

"Do not touch me! Go away immediately. Now!" I can not stop myself anymore. "You disappear forever from my life, just as you entered. I never want to see your face again, I do not want to hear never again your name!"

"Rebecca, please..."

"We will cancel the wedding, we will hurry up everything that will be done and disappear permanently. Did you understand me?"

Giulio nods. "I hope only you will be able to forgive me one day..."

"Get out. Now!"

I am on the verge of a crisis, and I fear that the situation can only degenerate.

"Addio Rebecca."

So saying, he comes out of the door and from my life.

After that evening we did not see each other

again. I asked my parents to take care of everything, since I would not have had that strenght.

A few days later I learned of his transfer to Milan, which had probably been decided for some. He often talked to me about his need to change the air, especially in the last period, since things with his father were getting more complicated due to some work divergences.

Apparently I was the last wheel of the cart for him.

Even now I struggle to understand what or who pushed him to leave me that way, and I can not help thinking that there might be another woman who had already taken my place in his heart.

In any case, my ex-boyfriend has always been a free spirit. He did not love very much certain relationship, and probably I should have aspect that sooner or later all this could have happened. Perhaps that was precisely the reason that had pushed me to insist so much for that marriage, putting him under pressure. In all probability, Giulio would never have asked me to marry him, because our relationship had always been good as it was, without too many restrictions. But I wanted more.

For four months I have been tormenting myself at the thought of having been so blind that I did not notice anything. I should have realized that something between us had been broken, perhaps saving me all the suffering that inevitably fell on my shoulders. But now it's too late, and certainly continuing to cry on me will not change the reality of things.

I can not remedy my mistakes, but I can at least try to get my life back on track. At least I owe it to myself.

I decide to go out to distract myself from too many negative thoughts. Take a bit of air can not be so bad, and in fact the sun was just a panacea. I was able to free up my mind and to feel a bit more lighter.

Probably Andrea at the end of all of this was totally right: a shake is what he really needs, but I need to understand what is going to be able to give it to me, and at this moment I don't have any idea.

7

The days are passing, each one identical of the other one, marked by the same rhythm that repeats itself like a chant.

This Sunday we have to go to lunch with my parents.

I go to them every 2 weeks, although I could and should show myself more often, but I prefer not to do this for obvious reasons.

One of the few reasons why I accept this torture is for the wonderful lunch that prepares my mother, a really excellent cook. I have inherited a lot from her in the kitchen.

Last night I prepared an apple pie, completely aware of hurting myself, having to suffer criticism that no doubt will rain on its part; but I hope at least will serve to distract everyone from the main topic of our conversations, or my ruinous life.

Preparing cakes relaxes me (even if I have to eat sweets, I risk losing weight!), and I am constantly looking for new recipes to experiment with. Sometimes, giving free rein to all my creativity, I replace or modify some ingredients, always creating something original, just like this time.

The second reason why I endure the torment of sunday lunch is my younger sister Ottavia.

She and I are very close, even if because of its many activities we can always see too little.

I get to my place at one o'clock, just in time to sit down at the table.

My mother knows that I do it on purpose, but she does not complain.

"Hello my darling!", welcomes me with a warm hug, which I exchange with affection.

"Hello mom. How are you?"

"I'm fine when I see you."

"You talk as if we had not seen each other for months" I say a little annoyed.

Why must it be so melodramatic?

"You look like an old maid!" she replies. "Can it become more intractable every day?"

My mother, in contrast to me, has the very bad habit of never being able to keep her thoughts to herself.

"Thank you so much mom. Always full of compliments!"

"So, you want to plant you two?", from the living room comes the voice of my father. "You are really dog and cat!"

I leave my mother in the kitchen and go to the dining room, where I find him already sitting at the table with Ottavia.

"Hello dad. Hello little sister" I say kissing both.

"How are you?" they ask me in unison.

"A wonderfull thing, as always" I answer not fully convinced.

"No news?"

"Nothing new and all of old" I say without giving too much weight to my words.

"You could also make you feel more often." From the kitchen comes yet another repramand. Is it possible that I never waste time to put myself in a bad light? I do not think I do it on purpose, I think rather than it comes spontaneous and natural, even if the reason for this behavior continues to elude me.

"Dear, do not harass her. Then do not complaint if she does not call me and doesn't come to visit us."

"You always ready to defend it, I recommend!", in her voice there is a fake note of disapproval.

"You are right mom", I admit to end the discussion. "I'm sorry. It's that..." I can not finish the sentence. I can not find words that can really express how I feel in this period of my life.

"But someone made a cake here, or I'm wrong?" Ottavia intervenes, managing to get me out of the embarrassment of the moment. She has always been my salvation and in any case manages to raise my spirits.

"Nothing escapes nothing, truffle dog!" I say doing the tongue.

Between me and her there are only two years of difference, even though I often still treat her as if she were the little girl of the house; but undoubtedly my sister knows very well how to defence herself, maybe even better than me.

Obviously as a child, even for us it was not only

affection and understanding, as for all the good sisters who respect each other. But growing up, and especially in recent years, our relationship is continuously improved, so much so that now we are not even a single day without feeling, even with a simple message.

Ottavia has certantly a certain carachter. Confident and not at all shy, it is my exact opposite. It's a tough girl, as I call it. She still lives with our parents only because it is the most convenient solution for her, and I can not certantly blame her; basically she gets on well with our mother, since she knows how to hold her head.

Physically then we resemble even less, if not for very few facial features. Ottavia infact is much smaller and thinner. Blonde, fair complexion, almost diaphanous, and green eyes, like mine. It could almost seem like an angelic figure, if we only focus on its outward appearance.

Going around with her has always caused me some discomfort. Since I was a child I have been taller than the average, and for this reason I tried to close myself up. My height was giving embarassement even though I was aware of having a lean and slender body, but because of my innate insecurity I refused to exalt.

Not to mention my hair: a real disaster compared to my sister's golden hair.

Brown, tending to rough and untamable, I have

always been my cross!

Lunch, unlike what I feared, passes quietly. My mother inexplicably, after the first initial bickering, no longer feels the uncontrollable impulse to put me under pressure and between a chat and the other, at the time of dessert, brings my cake to the table.

Everyone, even she, they agree looks delicious, and of course I hope it is also just as good.

"My God Rebbi, is really inviting!" exclaims Ottavia.

"Thanks little sister, but try before judging."

"Sure you did not put salt in place of sugar, right?" makes fun of me, knowing perfectly how much I can be touchy.

"But how you are witty! I could always decide not give you even a piece you know?"

"You would not dare!"

"You do not taste me."

We go on prancing ourselves, just like when we were children, even if now, unlike a time, we do it just for fun.

"Mmh..., excellent!" my father said, after putting a big piece in his mouth.

"Thanks dad. But you are biased. And then you would also eat the stones if they were only covered with sugar or chocolate!"

"It's absolutely not true!" he replies.

"Oh, yes it is", my sister gave me an hand.

"You are two ungrateful daughters!" exclaims pretending to be offended.

Ottavia and I burst out laughing.

My father is a sweet tooth, so I can never trust his judgment. Whatever I prepare, his opinion is always positive, unlike my mother's, which she manages to find every time something wrong: a pinch of salt in excess or one minute of cooking too much or otherwise too little. I do not think I've ever heard her say that a dessert of mine, or anything else cooked by me, was good; at least not before having demolished it with its countless negative comments.

Until some time ago I managed to gloss over hers criticism and let me slip on him, but now anything, even if minimal, manages to hurt me, and I do not understand why she does everything to turn every turn the knife into the wound.

His strange way of showing affection and concern towards us is sometimes exhausting to say the least. I know very well how much my mother loves me, but our differences and ways of doing things are certainly not what I need now.

Suddenly I feel the need to take a breath of air, so I ask Ottavia to go out for a walk.

I like spending time with my sister, only pity we can not do it more often. Octavia is in fact a very busy girl, even in the social, and then always has a thousand things to do, a lot of friends, and practice various types of sports.

Where do you find the time to do all these things for me is impossible to understand!

"How the work is going?" I begin the speech, to avoid questions that have me as subject. Although with my sister I know I can talk freely, I have no desire to discuss my life.

"Very well" she replies, but from her tone I realize that she feels almost uncomfortable in saying it.

"I am very happy for you my little sister." I am sincere, and obviously, despite my failure, I can not remaining wishing the best.

For some time, Ottavia has worked as a freelance photographer, with considerable disappointment from our mother.

That what started as a passion, and slowly become her job, despite he has been studying to become a teacher.

He had began taking pictures of events of all kinds: sports competitions, parties, the wedding of some friends, and so on, initially without receiving any remuneration.

Her is undoubtedly an innate talent.

On the day of her First Communion, as a script, she had been given a camera; same gift that I had received a couple of years before, but that had remained packaged and well closed in its packaging. Instead at Ottavia that same gift was liked very much, so much so that already that afternoon, at the restaurant, had begun to make pose of all the guests, almost stealing the trade to the official photographer.

She had a lot of fun taking pictures in the most inopportune moments, catching us by surprise, and with absurd faces, so that in the end it had become my torment, since I never liked being photographed. For this reason she, just to annoy me, secretly recovered, even during sleep.

One morning, not being able anymore, I stole her camera and threw it down from the balcony, pretending that it had fallen from my hands involuntarily. I still remember very well how Ottavia got mad at my gesture, and probably would have also gladly thrown me from the second floor if our father had not intervened to separate us.

In any case, even though as a child it was nothing more than a simple game for her, since then her remarkable abilities were evident.

With a simple *click*, she has always managed to capture details and capture moments, giving them her personal sense.

At the contrary of myself, she has been always a determined and decisive girl, and above all with the idea very clear about her life and about her future.

She had finished her studies and took her degree not so much to support the insistence of our mother, but to keep an open door in case things had not gone as she hoped.

"And you instead, what do you tell me?" Ottavia asks me, distracting me from my thoughts.

"Nothing worth talking about..."

"You do not have to break down Rebbi, you just have to have a little patience", she says trying to raise my spirits.

The same words that used also Andrea.

"Already" I simply replied.

"You would need to unplug the plug. It would surely do you good to go away for a while" she insists, even though I know well how I think about the subject. She had repeated that phrase more than once in the last few months and I never listened to it.

Sometimes I can really be stattborn.

I embrace her affectionately (of the two I am undoubtedly the most sentimental one), and we end our walk which is already almost dinner time.

I get my time to say goodbye, promising as always to make me feel and see more often, although we all know well that it is the usual promise that I will not keep.

When I come home I do not really want to eat.

Andrea left me a post-it attached to fridge:

CIAO REB. I STOP BY MARCO.
A KISS!

So I take a book in my hand, among the many borrowed from the library, and immerse myself in reading.

Reading catapults me into another dimension, as if I were in a parallel world.

I am a lover of romantic stories and happy ending. I hate the dramatic endings, and even more those who do not have a real epilogue, in which everything is left to the reader's imagination. I do not like in any way having to worry about the thought of what the author could or should have written. It's something I could spend hours and hours thinking about, given my cumbersome mind, in which I always give a single face and a well-defined identity to each character, so much so that sometimes they seem so real to me, that I think they can come out of the book and take possession of my apartment!

8

Another Monday morning.

Another week begins and in all likelihood will end just like the one just passed.

I have breakfast and I turn on the laptop. During the weekend I prefer not to look at job advertisements. It would really be too depressing.

I immediately go to the home page of the site to which I have recently registered, and I enter my credentials. After a brief search I read some news, but nothing that suits my case. Then I open the mail to check that there is not some company that has contacted me. But nothing here either.

It's all so daunting.

I send a message to Andrea.

Are you coming home tonight?

I really feel the need of his presence, and his answer does not wait.

Hi darling. Sorry, but also today I will stay by Marco.

Anyway we will get in touch later, agree?

Well, I'm hopelessly alone!

Even my best friend is leaving me!

I'm glad that the things between him and his new boy are going well, even if I have to admit I'm a little jealous.

I have to distract myself in some way, so I start surfing the internet without looking for anything in particular, but just to browse and spend some time. By doing so I end up casually in a site of ads of all kinds and I read them intrigued.

People write really about everything.

Some makes me smile, others leave me a bit shocker, then one of them cacthes me in particular:

WANTED GIRL OR BOY LOVE OF ANIMALS.
DYNAMIC WHAT HAS IT WANT AND TIME TO
DEDICATE TO MY BARNEY CUCCIOLONE, A
GOLDEN RETRIEVER.
GOOD REMUNERATION.

Wow, I did not think people could really need to entrust their dog to a dog-sitter!

I knew about this kind of work, but I considered it unlikely. Instead, this Cinzia, as signed in the announcement, seriously needs someone to care for her puppy.

Intrigued I begin to search the web for what you can earn with this type of activity, and to my surprise I realize that as a job is quite profitable -

especially for an unemployed like me - and does not commit a lot of time a day.

Suddenly I'm caught by an illumination: why not?

At the bottom of the animals I have always liked them a lot and as children my sister and I have had some: from parrots, to hamsters, to cats. In reality, never a dog, but all in all I think there can not be anything so complicated to handle it. Some strolls, a little pampering and fill a bowl of food and water.

I can do it!

I am convinced that this work can do for me, at least until I have found nothing more serious, and in any case could help me break the monotony of my days. And then I always wanted to have a dog.

So I decide to respond to the announcement, hoping to be contacted.

If my mother knew it would go crazy! "A girl with a university degree and with your skills, why should she waste her time paying attention to a dog?", here's what I would say.

I take a shower and go out.

I want to go to the park, and I bring something to eat with me. At this time there are many people who dine outdoors during the warm days of late September, enjoying the last flashes of sun, rather than remain closed in the office or in some local.

There are still those who do gymnastics, who runs along the bike path with the iPod headphones in their ears, who reads the newspaper sitting on the bench, and those like me can simply enjoy the warmth of the sun.

Meanwhile I am about to take a bite of my sandwich, I feel the phone vibrating in my jeans pocket. It is a message from an unknown number.

Hi Rebecca! I am Cinzia, the girl of the ad. Would you like to meet?
See you soon!

Damn! I did not think he would answer me, and above all so quickly. This is a good sign. I immediately write to you.

Hi Cinzia. It's great for me at any moment. Tell me where and when. And thank you for contacting me!

Another phone vibration.

I am on the Malaspina Gardens with Barney, she writes. *You could reach me here if it's ok with you. So you would also know my puppy*!

When we say the coincidence...

I'm here too!

Perfect! I wait for you at the entrance to the park.

You'll recognize me right away: right now I'm the only female of human race in the area!

This statement makes me laugh. Cinzia seems very funny.

So I walk towards the entrance.

When I find myself very close, I give a quick look towards the direction of the gate and see a girl tall, brunette, beautiful body and a tan practically perfect.

Tank top and black leggings highlight her slender line, and the hair are pulled in an equally impeccable ponytail.

She will have no more than twenty-three or twenty-four years, or he is shamefully less than he actually has!

I stop suddenly. In comparison to her, I'm unhappy, dressed at the least and with all the hair ruffled!

Thank goodness I should only look after your dog, which in case I hope you do not mind having a completely unkempt dog-sitter!

With her, however, I do not see any dog, but behind him, intent on sniffing the grass, instead known an enormous mass of hair.

Puppy?

That is a colossus of at least forty kilos, which right now, taken by some kind of sudden instinct, is throwing on his mistress making it almost fall to the ground!

She miraculously manages to maintain the balance, and I understand that that perfect body, as well as a lot of exercise, is surely due also by having to deal with a dog of that size.

I get closer, very curious. "You must be Cinzia."

"Yes, in person! Ciao Rebecca", she says giving me a quick look from the head to the toe.

I am convinced that she is already making a bad impression on me!

Instead she smiles at me and holds out my hand, and I hold her between mine. She has a nice, and very firm grip. It is immediately clear that this girl must have a strong personality.

"I'll introduce you to my puppy" she tells me. "But I warn you: keep yourself ready because it's a real tornado!"

I realized it, and I do not understand why she keeps calling him a puppy!

I look at her skeptically.

"Yes I know, it's not exactly small" says very sorry. "In reality it is already two years old, and it is at the height of its vivacity."

"In fact I expected a dog a bit more resized" I admit.

"I know it can scare you with its vehemence, but I assure you that it is very sweet and gentle. I just hope it's not a big problem for you."

"Well, actually not, but I want to be honest. I've never had a dog before, neither having to take care for one. I have a dwarf rabbit, and therefore it would be absolutely my first time doing this job."

I hope that my confession will not stop her relying on her dog. Sometimes I should be a bit less sincere and think more about my interests!

"Quiet" Cinzia tells me instead. "The only thing that matters to me is that Barney finds you funny, trust you and that you treat him as he deserves. I do not care about the rest."

At this point the subject in question came closer to me and begins to sniff me, like if he understoods our discussion.

"He likes you, I am sure. And you like to me as well!" she says.

"Thank you" I say a little surprised.

"Now that we've met, I'd like to better explain what I need."

"Tell me."

"The girl who occasionally deals with Barney she broke her leg last week, and consequently she will no longer be able to take care of him."

"I understand."

"In a couple of weeks I'll have to leave for work, and I'll stay away for more than a month" she explains. "Obviously he will not be able to come with me, so I need a person to take care of him during this time, and that he is willing to take him home with himself" she continues. "Would you have problems about it?" she asks me hopefully.

"Apart from my rabbit, which I do not think can be an obstacle, I think it can be done."

"Fantastic!" Cinzia esclaims enthusiastically. "I do not know who to entrust it to otherwise, and the time available to me to find someone is getting tight."

"Ok then, done deal" I say, content at least as much as her.

"In these weeks you may already begin to take care of him and take him on his daily walks, so you will learn to know each other. Anyway you will get along well together" she states convinced. "And it is obvious that I will also pay you for the disturb of these days."

"I can also start tomorrow if you want."

"Great!", now her satisfaction seems to be uncontainable. "Would you like a coffee?"

"Why not" I answer.

I already like Cinzia very much.

We sit at the tables at the kiosk and order two small coffees.

"What do you do in life?" she suddenly asks me. "Because I imagine that to be a dog-sitter is only a momentary makeshift, right?"

"Yes, actually it is", I answer got out-of-guard and with a bit of embarrassment. "I'm actually an interior designer. But I recently lost my job and like this for now I try to adapt myself."

"Really you are an interior designer?" she ask with a clear note of unbelief.

Okay, so let's pass the fact that right now I'm practically reduced to a rag, but this doesn't mean for sure that I can't even have an important and serious role in life!

I feel almost offended.

"Yes", I answer anyway. Adding also a: "Why?"

"Why you could be the right person for me?"

"Well, I already accepted to work for you", I also thought it was already clear.

"I do not mean Barney's dog-sitter."

"Ah no?", at this point I don't understand.

"On my return to Pavia I plan the move. Currently I live in a rented appartment" Cinzia specifies, "but I bought a new house and I would like that someone could take care of its fornitures. In fact I already had in mind to look for someone who could do it for me."

Suddently I lightens myself up.

"I understood" I only say, but inside of me I am already in seven heaven!

"I am completely denied for this kind of things and any I would not even have the time. You could take care of it, maybe, if you like."

Of course I like it, a lot!

Is something to ask?

"Yes, I think I can do it" I reply with demeanor.

"However, if at the end I feel satisfied with your work, I could also do some advertising. I have a lot of knowledge. What do you think?"

"I think it would be great!" I answer exultantly. "Thank you so much for the opportunity."

This would really be a great opportunity for me. Who knows that the wheel is not finally starting to turn in the right direction…

"I warn you: I am a very demanding person" she jokes.

"No problem. You're talking to a maniac of perfection."

"Well! Then you are hired for all!"

At this point, however, I'm intrigued, and I want to know something more about her. "And you? What do you do?" I ask.

"I am mainly a teacher of English literature, but I also work as a translator of novels and texts of various kinds for some publishing houses, both Italian and foreign."

I imagined he had an interesting job.

"You will travel often then" I say admired.

"Not as much as I would like. But it often happens to me to go abroad" confirms.

"I instead do not travel much…"

In fact I have visited several cities and regions of our country, but in all my life I have crossed the borders only a couple of times, and both with Giulio.

The third should have been for our honeymoon in Ireland, even the latter went up in smoke.

I stay to chat with Cinzia for about an hour.

It is very pleasant to talk with her, since she is a very outgoing girl and company, so much so that I almost feel sorry when she tells me she has another commitment. Anyway I go back home happy and full of expectations.

This day, which began like many others, turned out to be absolutely profitable.

I have a job, even in the very short term. But it does not matter. What really interests me is being able to finally be engaged in something, whatever it is. And then, in the meantime, I will also work on the project for Cinzia's new home, and this thought gives me a considerable positive dose. Also, if you will be satisfied with my ideas, this could broaden my future prospects, and finally, for the first time in months, I can not feel a total failure.

9

After weeks of doubts and uncertainties, I woke up this morning without the usual sense of restlessness, and I immidiately felt ready to face a new day.

Only twenty-four hours ago I responded to the announcement of an unknown girl and now I have a new job and new projects.

I immediately write a message to Andrea.

News coming..., I stay vague.

I'm sure it will not resist curiosity.

In fact, after not even one minute my cell phone starts ringing.

"Tell. What happened?" he asks me right away, without even say bye to me. "Have you maybe met the men of your life?"

"But stop it! No. Even better, I assure you."

I tell him about the story of the announcement,

and of my meeting of yesterday.

"Dog-sitter? And myself that I thought you have found the prince charming!"

"Come on Andy, be serious for once! And then you know very well that I no longer believe in fairy tales with an happy ending."

"And is not so good my dear. The happy ending always comes when you least expect it."

"I have to assume that the things between you and Marco are going pretty well, or I am wrong?" I ask smiling between myself.

"You can well say it! Never been better than that. But let's get back to you. The subject in question is not my love life now."

"I have already told you everything, there is not much to add. What do you think?"

"I think my hypothesis was much more tempting" he replies with a sigh. "But apart from that, if this can be a new opportunity for you, catch it on the fly. You know very well how I think about it. You are smart, beautiful, intelligent, you really do not miss anything to achieve your goals."

"Thank you. But you are biased."

"No. I am honest and I am always say what I think" reiterates.

"And that's why I've been entrusting to your advices for more than ten years."

I arrived at the park slightly in advance.

I have an apppointment with Cinzia at the fortheen and half, and after a few minutes of waiting I noticed that far there is a big dog is coming toward me.

Barney is undoubtedly.

"Ciao puppy!" I say carassing his head. "Happy to you again!" In response he turns me around making parties and claiming all my attention.

"He's already crazy about you! I knew I was not wrong."

"It's true, there is a certain feeling between us. Isn't true puppy?"

After taking a short walk together, Cinzia leaves me to go back to her job, entrusting her dog to my care. Suddenly, however, a thought assaults me: and if when I have to take him home, Barney began to chase Honey, and he would take a shock for the fright?

I certainly can not close Honey in a cage. I've never done it, except to take it on vacation or to the vet. He is not used to being closed, but to live free and roaring throughout the apartment, for seven years now. An absolutely enviable age for a rabbit.

I am very fond of him, and on the other hand he is the only thing that still keeps me tied to Giulio, since it was his gift for my twenty-third birthday.

At that time I wanted a pet very much. I wanted a dog, but Giulio considered it too demanding and then did not love dogs or cats much, in fact, he even said to be allergic. So the right compromise was a dwarf bunny.

I still remember very well the day when, returning from university, I found it at home locked in a cage, with a big red bow on top of it. That instant reminded me of the initial scene of *Lilli and the Wanderer*, when Gianni Caro gave his wife Lisa a tender cocker's litter for Christmas Eve.

I loved that cartoon as a child, and I have seen it millions of times.

Very happy for that unexpected surprise, I had hugged Giulio, and kissing him I could not stop thanking him. That all-white batuffolino was very tender and I was in love with it at first sight. So even the idea of having to do without him is unthinkable for me.

As I reflect on all this, suddenly the sky becomes black, and within a few moments it begins to diluge.

I just hope it's the usual late-summer storm that does not last long!

I look for shelter with Barney under the canopy of the kiosk but after five minutes the rain thickens further, and in the meantime my cell phone starts ringing.

I look at the display. It is Cinzia.

I answer.

"Ciao Rebecca" she greets me. "I hope you're not in the park yet."

"Well, honestly yes", in a regret way I admit.

This downpour was not really needed!

"If it does not stop raining, go to my house, it's closer. So maybe you'll get a little less wet."

"Ok. But how I do get the keys?" I ask her.

"Don't worry. You will find my brother. Now I warn him that you are about to arrive."

"Agree. Thank you."

"Imagine. No problem. However my apartment is on the forth floor" she specifies. "You already know the way."

I close the phone call.

Brother? I don't know for what strange reason, but for a moment I perceive the same feeling I felt yesterday when I met Cinzia: as it there was something unexpected and surprising waiting for me around the corner...

Meanwhile, it is continuing to rain incessantly and I see no other choice but to go to her house.

"Are you ready to get this shower Barney?" He looks at me, and as if is he has understood he begins to tug me. I start running to stay at his pace, but it is obviously much faster than me, which is nothing short of training.

We arrive in front of the gate of number 32 in less than two minutes, even if completely soaked.

Barney shakes the water off with a big jerk and if possible can soak my clothes even more.

I look for the surname of Cinzia among others on the intercom, and after having reread them all at least twice, the right one jumps to me.

I dial the number and immediately the door opens.

Since the apartment is on the fourth floor and I have no intention of going up by feet, I book the elevator.

During the wait I begin to wonder what the brother of Cinzia looks like, that undoubtedly is a very attractive girl. So I hope that he is not so, otherwise I will feel terribly embarrassed, especially for my appearance not entirely presentable at this time.

In fact, I take a quick look in the mirror and see the image of imperfection reflected!

A little bad. However, I could not do anything now, and then it is certainly not my fault if even the weather forecasts are on my side!

The elevator opens onto the fourth floor landing. I read the names on the doors and find what I'm looking for.

I ring the bell a couple of times and after a moment I hear the key turn in the lock.

Inexplicably I feel a little 'agitated, but above all I am not at all ready for the image that I find myself in front of me.

For a fraction of a second - which seems to me to be an eternity - I miss my breath.

It is not possibile!

I can not believe my eyes.

"Rebecca right? Come, come in as well" the figure in front of me tells me.

I mention a yes with my head, because I no longer use the word and I am almost in shock.

The person in front of me is none other than Sergio, the boy I was in love with for five years in high school, when I was still an ugly duckling that he enjoyed ignoring and mocking with his classmates.

We were not in the same section, but our classrooms were opposite each other, and during those years I had had eyes for him, like most girls in high school.

Sergio at the time could not have been defined otherwise than as the classic "beautiful and damned", since it fully reflected all the features. Intriguing and with an innate charm (which he knew how to exploit to his advantage), he was arrogant, presumptuous and impertinent, and he made fun of everyone, including teachers, always getting what he wanted. And as always happens with guys like him, he was obviously unattainable, especially for someone like me.

Now, more than ten years after the last time I saw him, that same person is one step away from me, and he is looking at me with the same identical eyes of that time. Black, deep and bewitching eyes.

I'm sure I'm not wrong, not on this look. It's really him, I'm sure.

I am completely dazed by the surprise of seeing him again, and I do not understand why he is continuing to look at me like that.

Maybe he recognized me, and he's trying to remember who I am. But suddenly I understand the real reason: without realizing it, I gave up the grip on the leash, and Barney, all dripping fur, literally fell into the house.

"Barney! Come over here right away!", Sergio is screaming. "Your mistress kills me if she finds the stained marble!"

I realize that the blame for his brusque intrusion at home is only mine, and I feel bloody embarrassed.

Worse than that it could not go!

I would like to be able to disappear, to eclipse from his sight.

"Sorry" I say, certainly already purple in the face. "I am very sorry."

I try to recover from that state of catalepsy, but I no longer know where to look to hide my discomfort and above all my face.

"Don't worry" Sergio tells. "But do not stay there on the threshold. Come in as well."

I can not avoid to notice that his stamp has changed, becoming naturally more mature, by a grown man.

"I would not like to disturb" I answer with a faint voice. "And then I'm all wet. I just had to bring

Barney back…”

I’m all wet?

I can not believe I just said this sentence!

I feel cheeks burning.

Even Sergio must have noticed my embarrassment more than obvious, because he says immediately: “Quiet. There is no problem. So now I’ll have to even dry anywhere thanks to that cyclone!”

And to me too, obviously.

“Anyway I am Sergio, the twin brother of Cinzia. Very nice to meet you Rebecca.”

Twin?

Of course, now I remember!

Sergio at school often mentioned his sister. I knew her name was Cinzia and also that they were twins, but I had never seen her before, so nothing could ever make me think of such an eventuality.

My interlocutor is holding out his hand, and I hesitate for a moment to hold it between mine.

I feel hot. His grip is strong and reassuring at the same time.

“My pleasure”, I reply.

Possible that he really did not recognize me?

Then he looks me straight in the eye and asks me: “We have not already met somewhere? You have a familiar face…”

Bingo!

“No. I don’t think so”, I lie without even realizing

it.

I do not understand why, but right now I can not tell him the truth.

Those of the high school, in some ways, have been very ugly years for me, and I certainly do not want him to remember that little girl with bottoms of bottle and the appliance on her teeth.

"Well, it is said that each of us has seven faces scattered around the world. Who knows, maybe I met one of yours!" he exclaims.

I smile in spite of myself at his joke, while his gaze continues to attract me like a magnet, just like ten years ago.

At this point I think it's better that I get out of here as quickly as possible.

"Do you want to stop for a drink? Or do you want to dry up first?" instead he asks me to displease me.

That? We joke?

Absolutely no!

"Thank you, but I have some things to do..." I reply quickly.

"But it is still raining very hard. Wait at least for it to stop. I think it will not last long."

"Thank you so much Sergio, but I really have to go."

I can not stay here a minute longer.

"However, I think at this point we will see each other very often. I currently live with my sister" he tells me spontaneously.

It 's true that at worst there is never an end therefore!

Should I see him again?

Not really talking about it!

I will tell Cinzia that I have reconsidered our agreement and that I can no longer deal with Barney.

Why the hell was she really Sergio's sister?

I greet him very hastily and I almost run out of the apartment, taking me down the stairs.

I do not understand why seeing him has made me such an effect.

Perhaps because it is the same person who made my heart beat and suffered at the same time for years? The one for which I have poured a sea of tears? Certainly not a trivial thing!

I go out of the door and breathe air with full lungs.

Until a minute ago I had almost felt suffocated and the past seemed to have fallen back on me like a boulder.

But why should misfortunes ever happen to me?

I want to go home. I can not wait to take a shower and wear clean and above all dry clothes.

On the way it finally stops raining - the only positive thing! - while I can not stop thinking about Sergio and of his penetrating eyes, and a shiver runs through my back.

I wonder how it can still provoke on me all these feelings. It will certainly be the fault of the fact that from my break with Giulio I have not been with a man, and I would have the hormones in revolt only for this reason. It was enough to see a nice guy and they are completely crazy!

A nice cold shower, even frozen, is the only thing I need.

10

It's eight o'clock in the evening.

Before dinner I decide to call Cinzia.

The phone rings a couple of times and then a male voice answers.

"Ciao Rebecca."

I recognize him instantly.

Why is Sergio ever answering his sister's cell phone?

"Ciao" I say.

"Cinzia has just left and forgot the phone at home."

What does he do? He reads my through now?

"Ok, does not matter. I did not have anything urgent to tell her."

"I will tell her to call you back."

"No really, it is not necessary. I will send her a message."

"All right, as you prefer. Good evening Rebecca."

"You too", I return.

I end the call and I call Andrea. I definitely need to hear his friend's voice.

"Hello? Rebbi?"

"You can not even imagine who I saw today!" break into, without even great him.

"Don't tell me that you met George!" he esclaims. "Why you did not call me right away?"

"Come on, do not be a fool! Unfortunately it was not George, but honestly it was much better."

"My darling, there is no one better than him, trust me that I am a connoisseur!"

"Anyway, I saw a person" I interrupt, just to further ignite his curiosity.

"Revised who? Come on, talk! What are you waiting for?"

"This is the brother of Cinzia, the owner of Barney. Do you remember the girl I told you about yesterday?"

"Go ahead", he presses me.

"Guess what? It is Sergio!"

I still feel a sense of fainting just by only pronouncing his name.

"Sergio who sorry?"

"But how? The boy I was in love with at the high

school, and who else! I was always talking about him, you can not don't remember him."

"Ah, so that Sergio", he says as he tries to get this person out of the maze of his memory.

"Right, exactly him."

"How small is the world!"

"Apparently... and you can not understand what a shock it was for me to see him again this afternoon."

"I can imagine... And him? He remember you?" he askes me.

"At the beginning no. Then he started asking me if we had not met before."

"And you what did you answer?"

"Obviously I lied! I could not tell him the truth. I was already too uncomfortable with the situation at the moment" I admit.

"Is it always as beautiful and impossible as ten years ago, or has it become fat and bald?" he asks me jocking.

"I wish was like that!" I sight. "Instead it is still terribly attractive. Indeed, perhaps in a certain sense it is even more so than before."

"So I guess you'll be forced to see it again."

"I really think so, whether or not. Unless I dump Cinzia, which I have already seriously thought of."

"And why should you do it? There is no reason" he reprimand me.

"Because I do not want to see him again, for no

reason!" I reaffirm decidedly.

In fact I really do not know what to do. I will have to work on the project for the home of Cinzia, as well as take care of her dog, so I would have to meet him very often.

"I do not understand why make it so tragic" Andrea insists.

"And you ask me too? Seriously do not you understand?"

Is it possible that Andrea does not realize what I feel?

"The only thing I understand is that you remained a girl, exactly like ten years ago!" he exclaims abruptly. "But what do you care about Sergio?" presses. "Did he make you suffer? So? You were in high school. And besides, you've never even been together."

This is true.

"Yours was only an adolescent infatuation, but it has passed water under the bridge since that time. Don't you think so?"

Reflecting about it, Andrea is completely right. I'm acting like a stupid teenager, but I've not been in a long time. I cannot give up the opportunity to work for Cinzia because of him. Giulio has already managed to destroy my life, and I will not allow anyone else to do the same thing.

"As always, your common sense has the best" I admit.

"Good girl. This is the Rebbi that I know!"

I finish to talk with Andrea and I would like to call again Cinzia, but the fear that the brother can still answer the phone makes me desist, therefore I sent her just a simple message.

Ciao Cinzia.
See you at the park tomorrow morning at half past eight.
Have a good evening.
Rebecca.

I eat a bite on the fly and go to bed, hoping to be able to fall asleep quickly, even if the business proves immediately more difficult than expected.

I keep turning around between the badsheets, unable to find the right position. I feel agitated and I can not reassure myself, until, at deep night, I finally abandon myself in the arms of Morpheus.

After almost a sleepless night, I get up restless, tired, and above all very unkempt, as if I had a fight with someone.

Of Andrea there is not even a shadow. By now it is already several nights that he is sleeping outside the house.

I do breakfast very fast, I dress up and I get out, even if it's not even eight o'clock in the morning.

After a long and lonely walk in the park, and

more than a quarter of an hour of waiting, there is still no sign of Cinzia.

I am about to write to her in order to know what happened to her, when from my shoulders I hear someone calling me.

Certainly it will be nothing but the fruit of my imagination and of a night passed without a close eye, but this voice can not be of Cinzia, nor a female voice, and unfortunately I think I know well who it belongs to.

I turn around and once again I find Sergio a few steps away from me, and once again I miss my breath.

But why did not I wear high heels and miniskirts this morning?

Maybe because I never wear the miniskirt, let alone the heels! And perhaps because it would not have been the most appropriate clothing for a walk in the early morning, in the park, with a dog!

It is official: I am going crazy.

"Hi Sergio" I salut him.

I am surprised to have found the breath to pronounce these two very simple words.

"Good Morning" he returns, giving me the same identical smile of the day before. "Cinzia was late this morning, so she asked me to bring you Barney."

How nice!

I will also thank you for this, as soon as I have way to see her!

"Ok" is the only thing I am able to say.

"Now I must go. See you soon Rebecca."

I like very much how he pronounced my name, how the sound of these few letters comes out of his mouth, almost like a melody, and I remain stolen.

NO! AND STILL NO!

I must not let myself be enchanted by him, nor by his persuasive voice.

"See you", obliged I answer.

"Ah, I forgot. Cinzia asked me to give you these", he says, pulling a pair of keys out of his jeans pocket.

Grasping them I feel a jolt going along the back to the simple contact with his fingers, and I remain almost paralyzed. I look at him and he seems to be perfectly at ease.

It seems obvious to me!

A person like Sergio does not break up because of such nonsense, as opposed to a sentimental like me.

"Thank you" I mumbled.

"Thanks to you and have a nice day", he says waking me up from my momentary state of trance.

I'm already leaving, when he insists: "Yet I still think I've already met you. What a strange thing don't you find it?" he asks me displacing me.

"Right. But I'm sure I've never seen you before." Lying seems to have become almost natural for me now.

We say goodbye once again and finally everyone

goes his way.

What a situation!

I absolutely do not want Sergio to recognize me. I could not bear it. It would remind me of the bad moments I spent in high school, when I felt like a fish out of water. When my only thought was addressed to him, the most beautiful boy I had ever seen. When to not think I dive into the study, isolating myself from the rest of the world day after day, after day...

The years of high school for me have not been happy at all and I do not keep a good memory, if not for a few companions and some teachers. I have never felt at ease among those school desks, but always just inadequate.

All my energies and my time I was spending it on books. I did not frequent many people outside the school context, and apart from very rare occasions, I did not go out so often.

No disco, no afternoons at the park with friends, no motorbike rides, and especially no boy. Nobody considered me pretty enough to get with me, even if I doubt I would have liked anyone else who had not been Sergio.

I was very similar to a hedgehog closed at ball and full of spiky quills.

Not that in all these years it changed very much then...

Sometimes my life weighed on me, but I was so

used to living it as it was that I rarely could imagine it different. Perhaps I did not even care that it was, and on the other hand I would not have been able to dress other clothes if not mine.

But I was aware that things would one day change and that I would have pulled out my wings, finally taking off my flight.

Pitty that the flight was so short!

Barney seems very happy to see me and does a lot of parties to prove it to me.

"Why Sergio manages to make me feel this way again?" I ask him, even if obviously I'm just asking myself.

He first looks at me with his sweet eyes, then invites me to play, distracting me for a few moments from my perplexities.

We walk for a while along the tree-lined avenue of the park. Barney occasionally pulls me to throw himself in chasing of a sparrow, a butterfly or anything else flying

After an hour and a half passed in this way, I decide to bring it back home.

We enter the apartment of Cinzia and take off the leash. This gesture immediately reminds me of what happened only a day ago.

I go to the kitchen, I take a bowl from the ground and I pour the content in the sink, then filling it with fresh water that Barney immediately rushes to drink.

"Good puppy. Now you're good. See you this afternoon, okay?"

I'm about to leave, but taken by curiosity I decide to take a quick look at the rest of the house.

It is not very large, but still comfortable, even if you notice immediately that those who live there do not have too much time to dedicate to the house.

The kitchen is divided from the living room by an arch ending with a low brick wall. The colors are very sober and the minimal furniture, modern and light tones.

I think that with a touch of style both the kitchen and the living room could become more welcoming and take on a more airy look. Spaces currently appear much smaller than they actually are, but with the right care you could create two environments that look a lot wider.

While I make these considerations my attention is captured by a photograph place in a frame on a shelft.

He portrays two children playing on the beach. They look happy and smile, splashing each other's water.

In those smiles I can not fail to recognize Cinzia and Sergio, because they are still identical to those of the past, and this makes me a certain effect. I notice only now how much they resemble, even now that they have become adults.

I'm staring at the picture for a few moments, then suddenly feeling me of too much I regard Barney and I leave from the apartment.

On my way back I send a message to Cinzia to tell her that I will be back to her house in the first afternoon.

I prefer not to mention of my meeting of yesterday with her brother, nor of this morning, but for my back luck will be her to do it for me.

So, what do you think of my big brother?

More direct than this could not have been! Cinzia is a person too spontaneous, but I do not understand what you expect me to answer.

I think she is aware of the fact that her brother is a handsome guy, and also very attractive. What she doesn't know, and let alone imagine, is that I've known him for a long time...

Sergio was really kind, I just respond, not really knowing what else to add and hoping she does not insist on the subject.

In the afternoon I decide to bring Barney to me, wishing only to not make a mess, since in trouble I have always been a true expert.

Not knowing where Honey is, and certainly not

wanting him to take a heart attack, I cautiously enter. But the new arrival starts immediately to sniff everywhere perceiving his smell.

I just hope he does not decide to hunt him now!

While I continue to firmly tighten the leash for fear that it might escape once again from my hand, he stops, straightens his ears, fixes a point in front of himself and pulls me hard.

Spotted prey!

Honey, felt the danger, goes to take shelter readily under the sofa, and I not hardly drag the dog into the bathroom, but immediately he begins to scratch bchind the door in protest.

Perfect, now it will certainly scratch!

Unfortunately I have no other choice. I must first recover Honey and try to reassure him. Although initially it proves suspicious, because it smells on me the smell of the intruder, with a little patience - and some salad leaves - I make it in my attempt. I take it in my arms and go to the bathroom door, behind which the recluse began to bark insistently. I open it with caution and giving it a quick glance I immediately realize the damage.

"Thank you very much Barney!" I said a little upset. "Now I will have to repaint it." But this is certainly not the time to think about it. Infact I do not manage to sidestep that he has already jumped on me, and my rabbit rabbit is splashed away like a rocket, with the puppy in his chasing.

I'm really a genius!

And now what do you do?

Somehow I take back that tornado of a dog on a leash, while Honey managed to get under the couch again, where the big paws of his pursuer can not reach.

Slightly upset I call Cinzia, who after a few rings luckily answers.

"Hi Rebecca. Is everything all right?" she asks right away.

"Ehm…, sincerely not really …" I am forced to confessed.

"What happened?" she asks alarmed. "Did Barney escape while you were at the park? Did he bite someone by chance?"

"No, don't worry. Nothing of all this" I reassure her.

"Thanks God", she sights.

"The truth is that I brought him to my house. But it was a real disaster!"

"Really? I am sorry."

"The problem is that now Barney seems crazy and I do not know what to do."

"Ok, do not worry. You will see that we will find a solution before I leave. Actually, I think I already have something in mind…"

"Perfect!" I exclaimed heartened. "Any idea is well accepted."

"I could send Sergio to your house, with Barney.

We really can do with him, and I would see that he will be of great help."

Here we go, maybe any other idea except this one!

Immediately I think of the eventuality of having to see Sergio again, and moreover at my house. Argument to say the least out of the question!

Cinzia instantly perceives my moment of perplexity.

"Don't worry, doesn't bite!" she says laughing.

"What?" I asks a bit dazed. "Of course not!" I say recovering and trying to seem indifferent. "It's just that I would not bother him for such nonsense. And then it will certainly have better things to do..." I say, hoping with all myself that he really can be like that.

"For him will be a pleasure give you an hand."

"If you say so...", I reply not very convinced.

"I'll tell him to come to you as soon as he has time. Always that you agree, of course."

No I don't agree! I wish I could tell her. "Very good then", instead I have to answer.

It is really true that disasters never come alone!

11

This morning I decided to wear overalls and sneakers. I'm serious about trying to get back into shape, just like Andy suggested to me, who obviously will never convince to keep me company. But I will take advantage of my walks with Barney (which fortunately is a great distraction and helps me not to think about anything), to do a little jogging, although initially I'll have to go slowly, since I'm completely rusty!

Barney seems to have liked this initiative right from the start, and he is at my pace, which at first is very slowly slowly taking the right pace, starting to increase more and more.

It seems very happy to run alongside of me, and I think he's used of doing it with Cinzia. Undoubtedly she is a girl who takes a lot of her physical appearance.

I brought the mp3 with me, and I have music blaring in my ears. I feel free, as I have not felt for some time, and this feeling gives me a strong energy.

I run, breath, run, breath.

I feel only the beating of my heart in the chest and the notes of the songs that seem to want to mark my steps.

In front of me there is nothing but the tree-lined avenue.

I'm alone with myself. Only me, simply Rebecca, without bad thoughts to cloud my mind, while my pace is even faster.

I like running, and I wonder why I never decided to do it before.

"Thanks Barney. It's all about you, you know?" I ask him, but I immediately realize that he is not at all looking after me.

In fact, suddenly stops, points his big paws and does not want to learn to continue.

I don't understand what has been happening to him.

Then I turn to the direction in which he is looking and I see a dog completely identical to him who runs on the lawn in front of us. From his reaction I deduce it is a female.

"Come on puppy, let's go!", I try to pull him towards me, but Barney does not at all seems inclined to want to follow me.

"Come on!" I insist, without any result.

"I don't think he is so willing to follow you."

I was so intent on distracting Barney from his vision, that I was not the least bit aware of the guy who approached me, and that he obviously must be the owner of the other golden retriever

"She's Milla" says pointing at her. "I instead are Lorenzo."

I look at him a bit annoyed.

"Rebecca" I introduce myself, even if I do not give a damn about making this acquaintance.

This break was not planned, and I just want to be able to resume my race.

"Ciao beautiful", he says, turning to Barney, who immediately, feeling in the center of attention, suddenly turns and jumps on him, dragging me along with him.

"Sorry, I'm mortified" I say giving myself a

demeanor. "When he behaves like this, I can not just hold him back."

"I'm used to it, don't worry", he smiles at me.

"I imagine..." I say pointing out with the look at his dog.

"You are a pretty big dog, aren't you?" he continues caressing Barney, that in response lies down with his belly in the air to receive his dose of pampering.

"I could give you some advise if you want. On how to teach him, I mean."

"In reality it is not my dog. I'm just his dog-sitter", I precise.

"Oh really?" he asks me as if he did not believe what I just told him.

"Exactly. Anyway now we really have to go. It was a pleasure" I hurried short cut. "Come on Barney, let's go now!" I command in a firm tone, hoping to be able to make it walk. But moving forty kilos of dog, which moreover has no intention of moving a single step, is not an easy undertaking at all.

"I think Milla likes him a lot. It could be love at first sight" he jokes, and I know he really has a big smile. But otherwise I do not think much of it. Anyway he and his dog are making me lose a lot of time.

I'm really very annoyed, so I pull Barney to me with all the strength I can find and he finally, even if reluctantly, decides to follow me.

"Good continuation" he tells, the guy of whose name I have already forgotten.

"You too" I answer out of politeness.

"Maybe we will meet again. Me and Milla come here every morning."

"Could be then" I find myself forced to say this, even if I sincerely hope not.

We only lacked Barney in heat and the guy who wanted to give me advice on how to train him. Of course! Just a nice sly excuse!

Probably I should feel flattered, but his intrusion irritated me, and not a little.

"Did you see what you did?" I ask Barney earnestly, looking at me with those languid eyes, as if he understood what I just said and was seriously disappointed.

"I'm kidding. You're very good, do not worry" I say caressing him, and carrying our running.

After almost two hours of training I am really exhausted.

Maybe I have a little exaggerated to be only the first day, but despite the physical exhaustion, after a shower I feel already regenerated.

I immediately write a message to Andrea.

I went running this morning.
And you, when do you think to come with me slob?

I'm nothing short of hungry, so I prepare two toast with tomato and salad, and I devour them in a moment. I just hope that running does not make me the opposite effect!

Without an apparent reason I remember the boy I met in the park. How did he say he was called? Of course I'm a real disaster with names! I can never keep them in mind. Anyway doesn't matter very much anyway, even if I see him again I'm not obliged to remind his name. And then it seemed a strange type, as well as very intrusive, and I hope not to have to cross again on my way.

While I still await a response from Andrea, I receive a message from Cinzia. She warns me that Sergio will pass by me in the late afternoon.

Damn! I'm trapped!

I'm not at all ready to receive him in my house. However, it is still four o'clock in the afternoon and I have plenty of time to make myself and my apartment presentable for his arrival, even if I do not see the reason at the end, since it is certainly not a gallant appointment. But regardless of the nature of our meeting, I do not like it being caught unprepared, so I start to reorder here and there.

Being a freak of order, however, I lose more time than expected, and since Andrea is my exact opposite, I have to put in place even the things that he left scattered throughout the house.

If he would matter to take care of my apartment as much he takes care for his own person, without any doubt the first one would be a mirror!

Normally his chronic disorder does not weigh me, since for Andy I would do anything, even if most of the time tends to take advantage of it. But right now if I had it in my hands I could even strangle him!

At six forty-five minutes I realize that the house shines, but I am a real disaster, and above all, I have not had enough time to fix it.

I run to the bathroom to give me a refresh.

I would like to put on some makeup, but Sergio will be here at any moment. So I put on a sweater and a pair of clean shorts, I put my hair in order and after a few minutes the intercom rings.

It's obviously him.

Perfect. Another maniac of punctuality!

At this moment I do not find it exactly as valuable as it might seem on a different occasion.

"Come upstairs", I tell him. "Second floor."

Now I can not pull back.

12

Tense as the string of a violin and nervous to the tip of the hair, I go to open the door.

When Sergio sees me he gives me one of his usual

breathtaking smiles. "Hi Rebecca. How are you?" he cordially asks me.

"Hi Sergio. Fine, thank you. And thank you for your disturb, but your sister insisted very much..." In truth I let myself be convinced quite easily I would say!

"Do not worry, I'm glad to give you a hand, if I can."

Something meanwhile is rubbing against my leg, and of course I realize that it is Barney's nose.

I was so distracted by Sergio's closeness, that I completely forgot about his presence, which is the reason why both are here.

"Hi puppy", I say caressing him, while he shows me his love by licking me.

"Apparently he likes you a lot" Sergio observes.

"And he likes me", I sincerely admit, and suddenly I realize that we are still on the threshold of the entrance.

"Pardon me" I say moving from the door. "Come in."

The usual bum!

"Where is your furry friend?" he asks me.

My furry friend? Nice appellative. I like it.

"I locked him in the bathroom before you arrived" I answer. "I did not want him to be scared again like this afternoon. It is very delicate, and can not undergo strong emotions" I explain.

"Ok. Then we must try to do things gradually, so

that it can get used to Barney's presence."

"Right" I confirm, thinking about how stupid and unwise I was just a few hours ago.

"By the way, I have not asked you what it's called yet."

"Honey. It's called Honey."

"Honey... Just a sweet name there is nothing to say."

For a moment his eyes meet mine, and they are so penetrating that I almost bare myself.

I immediately turn red in the face and immediately distract my gaze.

"Are you ready?" he asks me.

"Yes", I answer a little 'uncertain.

"Ok then go ahead and get it. I'll wait for you here."

I can not yet believe that this situation is real: me and Sergio alone, in my house!

I am torn between the impulse to send it away as quickly as possible and to keep it here forever, even if now I should only think to mitigate the hostility between our two four-legged friends.

I open the bathroom door very carefully. I want to avoid that Honey goes in alarms and runs away once again. Instead I find him to doze. So I take it in my arms and go to the living room; but as soon as he sniffs in the air the presence of another animal stiffens, and begins to agitate. I try to hold it close to me and very calmly I approach Sergio and

Barney, who immediately starts barking in my direction.

Slowly I sit on the carpet, with Honey more and more afraid in my arms. Sergio approaches us putting his hand in front of his nose, and he immediately begins to smell it intrigued.

He is still on the alert, but fortunately Barney has stopped barking, perhaps reassured by the presence of a person who knows better than me, and so Honey too is reassured.

"Well it was not that difficult" he tells me a few minutes later. "They will become inseparable, you will see."

"Yes you are right. I was really stupid this afternoon" I admit.

"I would say simply not very careful." He smiles at me, and I'm forced to look away once again.

"I seem to understand that you like animals a lot", almost stutter because of the disturbance that causes me this circumstance.

But why I talk endlessly, instead of making sure that he goes away?

"In fact I love everything that has four legs and hair in abundance, moist nose and an infinite need to give and receive love."

From his words, I hardly recognize him. He does not even seem like the old person anymore.

"Can I offer you something to drink?" I ask him

writhout thinking.

I must seriously lose my mind!

Why can not I be a little quiet?

"Thank you, but I think it's better that Barney and I we shove out of here..."

"No trouble, in fact, it is the least I can do, since you took all this trouble for me."

"I have already told you: it is not a problem, and you must not in any way feel in debt."

"I would still be pleased if you would accept my invitation..."

But where did all this shamelessness come from? It is not really from me to be so blatant!

Please Sergio tell me no! TELL ME NO!

"Well, if you insist, I gladly accept."

I knew it! Here's a perfect way to get into trouble with your own hands!

Surely I must have stopped to rationally think the moment I saw him again.

"Take a seat", I say pointing at the sofa'.

The only thing I can do at this point is to hope that the situation does not completely escape my control.

"Cinzia mentioned to me that you take care of interior design", he starts. "I believe it's a job that has to give you a lot of satisfaction."

It seems obvious to me that his sister must have told him about me.

"Yes" I answer, and if I still had my job I could

also call myself fully gratified!

"And what exactly do you do?"

His obvious interest destabilizes me.

"Well, I deal with furnishing and revisiting the enviroments, wheter it's apartaments, offices, shops of any other kind of room. I try to make them cozy and inviting, to give them a touch of style, of personality, and above all of color. The monotony in my work is the first thing to be banned."

"Really interesting" he sincerely states. "I know that you will also take care of the new house of Cinzia."

"Yes, infact" I confirm. "I will first have to look at it to study its spaces and also understand its tastes and needs."

"You'll have a good deal to do then. I hope you know" he says laughing. "My sister is a girl with difficult tastes."

"She already confessed it to me. But will not be a problem" I say honestly. "I'm used to dealing with many types of customers, from those that are intractable and extremely demanding, to those that are more easily satisfied. And then the challenges in the workplace do not scare me", at difference of those sentimental ones, I would add.

He looks at me almost admired. "You're a smart girl, you can see right away", flatters me.

This topic starts not to like me. I prefer not to talk about myself, because I already feel the earth give way under my feet.

"And you instead, what do you do?"

Apart from having the real need to change the subject, I am seriously curious to know something more about his life, especially because I can not really imagine what career he has been able to undertake over the years.

For what I remember, in high school he had never shone for his vows, nor did he boast of a good reputation as a student. The only subject in which he always excelled was gymnastics, and observing it even now it is easy to guess why, given his statuesque physique.

"I can tell you for sure that even in my work you need a good dose of passion, creativity and patience" he then explains, thus increasing my interest.

"Are you suggesting me a riddle?"

"I could, it would be fun, but I'll make it easier for you. I am a chef" he finally declares.

Sergio a chef? I think it is absolutely the last thing I would have thought about, and I am particularly amazed.

"Really?" I ask still wondering.

"Yet" he confirms. "Although I must admit that for me it is a vocation rather than a job."

"And from what does this vocation come from, if I may ask?"

I would like to be able to find out as much as

possible about this new Sergio that I still do not know and that intrigues me in an almost morbid way.

"To ask is permitted" he replies courteously. "Anyway, I inherited it from my uncle, my mother's brother." In his voice I almost hear a note of emotion.

"You must be very fond of him" I dare.

"Yes, I was. Unfortunately he died last year."

"Oh, I am sorry."

"For me it was like a father, in fact, I can say that he was closer to me than my mother's ex-husband...", he stops.

I would not want to reopen old wounds with my questions, because I clearly perceive his suffering, and I regret having done so, even if unintentionally.

I do not know what to say, and the silence is suddenly becoming heavy.

"Just think that today I discovered my vocation for running!" I exclaim, risking to seem silly and frivolous, but not knowing how else to get him out of his momentary muteness.

Unexpectedly, however, he makes a smile, and his eyes return to be bright as a moment ago.

"My passion is basketball" Sergio says, recovering from his moment of emotion.

"I instead never had a great predisposition for sport" I confess. In fact, at school the hours of gymnastics were a real nightmare for me, and when

I had the opportunity I tried in every way to avoid them.

"Are you a professional?" I ask him.

"Unfortunately not, but in the little free time I have at my disposal I train a female team under 18."

Really admirable.

"And so you're a coach."

"I try" he answers. "Although I prefer to call myself an instructor" he spericifies. "I like being in contact with teenagers, perhaps because in this way I can stay attached to the boy who is still in me." He pauses and then adds: "Does it seem solly?"

"Not at all. Instead, I find it a very beautiful thing."

"Yes it is, even if it makes me uncomfortable to talk about it."

He, Sergio, feels uncomfortable?

But what happened to the guy I knew? Almost no trace left!

"You shouldn't" I say very stably. "It's nice to dedicate some of your time to others. And then in this way your life does not risk becoming monotonous."

Surely it is not only compared to mine!

First Giulio, then the job. A failure after another. Instead, its existence gives the impression of being intense and fully lived.

"In fact it is so, and it does not weigh on me. It is

for this reason that Cinzia has sought someone to entrust with Barney. I would not have had much time to dedicate to him" he justifies himself.

"Have you been living with your sister for a long time?" I continue with my interrogation.

"For a few months already. Although in reality I am only a guest, and I will continue to be in her new home as well" he says ironically.

I would like to know why, but I do not think I should ask other personal questions. I would not want him to be bothered by my intrusiveness, despite my curiosity is more than legitimate.

I've known Sergio for fifteen years, but in reality I do not really know anything about this person who in the meantime has completely changed, making the bourgeois and bully boy of the past disappear. Even his smile seems to have softened, but remains damn fascinating. Perhaps too much!

I realize that I could remain seated on this sofa to admire his thin and perfect lips forever, if it were not that suddenly I remember his words a moment ago, when he mentioned the adolescent that still dwells in him, and I am shaken by a slight shiver.

Since we are sitting very close, even Sergio must have perceived it.

"Are you cold?" he is asking me infact.

"No. Must be a bit of tiredness", I lie. "I am curious. How were you at the time of high school?" I ask following an irrepressible instinct.

It's official: I'm not only crazy, but also particularly masochistic!

But now the words come out of my mouth uncontrolled, as if I were no longer me to pronounce them.

"Your interest flatters me" he jokes. "I can simply tell you that during the high school years I was a very presumptuous and full-blown boy. A real idiot!"

Really? I knew it very well!

Too bad only that I can not confess it to him.

"If you had known me then, you would almost certainly have hated me" he carries on.

"I can hardly believe it…"

This is true. Despite everything I would never have been able to hate him. Inevitably, however, his words bring back a bad memory from the past…

13

I'm in the school yard.

It's a beautiful day at the end of May. The school year is about to end and the exams for maturity will start soon.

I'm intent on lifting the chain from my bike, while a few steps away from me there are Sergio and Alessio, his best friend and my classmate, both of course completely unmindful of my presence.

"Hi" I greet them with my head down.

"Ah, hi…" Alessio answers in a distracted, almost annoyed tone.

"Mamma mia, how ugly she is!" Sergio exclaims under his breath, but not enough not to be heard. "I could never kiss a girl like that. Or maybe only in my worst nightmares!"

They both start laughing, and that little bit of hope, though minimal, about the fact that maybe one day the boy of my dreams could have noticed my existence, has been shattered. It has dissolved, vanished, annihilated, destroyed! And with me also my wretched and fragile heart.

A punch in the middle of my stomach would surely have done less harm than the blow that Sergio, unbeknownst to me, has just inflicted on me.

The tone with which he pronounced his words was terribly crue. But maybe I am wrong. They are right. Maybe this Rebecca, a melancholy and insignificant girl, that nobody could ever accept, should simply disappear, to make room for a new awareness...

"Are you sure you are doing fine?" Sergio is asking me.

I have a jolt. That memory can still hurt me today.

"Yes. What were you saying?"

"Maybe it is better that I go..."

In fact I think so too, although it is still very early and in reality I have not yet given him anything to drink.

"Excuse me so much, I did not mean to be rude to you. But stay, please."

He stares at me for the umpteenth time.

I do not understand why he has this very bad habit!

"Do you believe in reincarnation?"

What kind of question is this?

"I don't know" I answer. It is certainly not a subject to which I often think.

"I believe that our souls after death continue to wander in a sort of limbo, until they find the right body to relive once again..." Is interrupting himself, as it to reflect on the concept that he wants to express, then resumes: "I still think we may have met in a previous life" he says seriously. "Does it seem possible?"

A previous life?

Who knows, maybe it really was...

"Or we may have attended the same schools", insists.

"I do not think it is possible!" I exclaim with more emphasis than necessary.

I'm afraid that at any moment I could be swallowed up by the pit that I myself am digging under my feet.

"It could be a valid hypothesis ...", he continues.

"I moved to Pavia only after university, so I'm afraid it's not possible."

I'm lining up one lie after the other, but I can not avoid it anymore, and unexpectedly I realize I'm even too easy to say.

"Would you like a juice, or a cold tea, maybe?", I take this opportunity to close the topic. "Sorry, but I have nothing alcoholic at home. Me and my roommate are both teetotalers."

Pronouncing this sentence I can not avoid but notice his expression. It is absurd, but it is as if it had bothered him to become aware of the fact that I share my apartment with another man. But in all likelihood it was only the projection of what I would like to prove to me: that is, a touch of jealousy.

"So you don't live alone?" he asks me then, giving

an additional imput to my thought.

"No" I confirm. "For some time I have been living with my best friend, Andrea."

Am I wrong or have I just seen him breathe a sigh of relief?

What idiocy!

For sure it will have been just another projection!

"You know each other since a while?"

His curiosity is confusing me.

"Since ten years" I say in a short cut. "But you have not yet given me an answer…"

He looks at me without understanding what I am referring to.

"You still have not told me what I can offer you to drink."

What am I doing? I should try to send him away from here, instead of continuing to hold him back, although it is very pleasant to have a conversation with him.

"Ah, yes, sure… A glass of icecold tea will be fine. Thank you."

"Perfect" I say. "Stay comfortable here as well. I'll be back in a moment."

"I have to stay calm. I have to stay calm. I have to stay calm!" I keep repeating myself like a mantra.

After all, I only invited him to drink something, nothing more. We'll talk a little more, and then he'll leave. There is really nothing to worry about. Or at least that's what I hope.

I go into the kitchen, I open the dishwasher and take two glasses.

Looking in the refrigerator, however, I realize I have not put the tea in the fresh air.

What a spurious breed!

I then take a container and retrieve a few ice cubes from the freezer. Lay it all on a tray and head into the living room.

Barney and Honey are dozing next to each other. I had not even realized it, and I have to admit once again that it was really very good. Probably at this time I would still be trying to find a solution!

But in observing them I distract myself a second, just enough to make me raise my foot too little and stumble across the carpet in front of the couch.

The tray literally flies into the air, and I fall ruinously at Sergio's feet.

14

It's a sunny and warm day in early spring.

I love this time of the year and it is absolutely my favorite.

The awakening of nature from the long winter hibernation, the inebriating perfume of the blooming flowers, the warmth of the sun that begins to warm the skin... It is as if I awakened myself from a long sleep.

I'm crossing the street just in front of the entrance gate of the *Art High School R. Sanzio*, my school.

I raise my head to let me caress my face from the warm rays of the sun, but this carelessness costs me a lot. I do not realize I have the sidewalk immediately in front of me and I stumble, ending up on the ground.

Immediately I find myself with forty eyes focused on, but obviously no one rushes to give me a hand to get up. So I pull myself up as if nothing had happened, and purple in the face trying to regain a minimum of behavior.

I look at my legs and realize that I have torn my

jeans, as well as having my left knee completely scratched and that it is starting to burn slightly.

I would like to become transparent, invisible, even if in a certain sense it seems that I already are.

Everyone looks at me amused, laughing at my shoulders, and among them I can not help but notice the presence of Sergio.

I feel like dying.

He is also making fun of me like everyone else.

I try to put myself together and pretend nothing has happened. I do not really know if at this moment the scratches are more burning, or my pride hurts.

Only Martina, my best friend (or rather the only friend that I have), tries to help me handing me a handkerchief.

"Are you okay?" she asks me.

I do not know what to answer her. Physically I think so, apart from the knee, but inside me there is nothing that goes well!

"Is all fine, thanks" I anyway answer her.

Martina is one of the very few people with whom I get along and with whom I managed to make a bond in these five years.

Sometimes in the afternoon we meet at her house to study together, and I think she is the only one not getting ashamed of spending time in my company.

"Is it all finen Rebecca?" This time, unlike many

years ago, Sergio is the one asking for it.

"Yes, all fine", or at least I think so.

He gives me his hand and helps me get back on my feet.

"What a disaster!"

Tea spilled on the carpet, a glass shattered, and Sergio's jeans were wet!

Damn me!

Why am I always so clumsy? An elephant in a crystal shop would certainly do less damage than I can do by simply raising a finger!

"Do not worry. Now I'll help you clean up."

"No, do not bother" I say. "I dry everything in a moment. I'm just sorry for your pants." I am really mortified.

"Imagine nothing serious or irreparable happened."

For me yes!

"If you want to go to the bathroom to dry off, it's as if you were at home."

It can not be true!

I can not have done this bad picture, exactly like ten years ago!

Fortunately, Sergio seems to be another person but who knows what he will think of me now.

While I'm bent over the carpet trying to clean up everything, I hear the front door open.

"Hi dear" Andrea greats me. "But what are you doing?" he asks, looking first at me and then at the shards of the glass still scattered on the floor.

"A small incident...", caused by my ineptitude!

"Rebecca, where I can find the hair dryer?" from the bathroom comes the voice of Sergio. "I would not want to rummage among your things" he adds.

"Look in the white piece of furniture, the one above the sink" I answer.

Andrea looks at me with a huge question mark printed on the face. "Who is in the bathroom?" he asks me mischievous. "I see that during my absence you have been busy, clever!" he exclaims.

"What are you saying? It's not like you are thinking! And lower the voice please!" I admonish him. "Sergio came here just to give me a hand with Barney and Honey."

"Sergio?"

"Yes, exactly."

"Have I missed something?"

"You have not lost anything. I just told you: he came here just to help me" I repeat. "But then I made a mass, as usual!"

"What happened?" he asks, raising his eyes to the sky, accustomed to my continuous gaffes.

"I stumbled on that damn carpet, and I blew the tray in the air that I had in my hands."

He bursts out laughing.

"You're the usual! I imagine the scene..."

"I can not find anything funny! Stop laughing!"

Sergio meanwhile comes out of the bathroom and

Andrea immediately goes to meet him to introduce himself.

"Glad Andrea, the roommate of Rebbi!" he says, holding out his hands.

"Sergio. My pleasure."

"I know you, Rebbi told me about you."

"Ah, really?" curious question.

Andy you're a traitor! You pay me this!

"Do you stop with us for dinner?" he asks him then. "I was in you I would accept. Rebbi cooks divinely. It's the main reason why I endure living with her" he jocks.

If he does not stop immediately, I swear I'll shut his mouth with the first thing that I find!

Instead of helping me it's making things even more complicated, as if they were not already enough.

"I think I've already made him waste enough time tonight. Surely he will have better things to do..." I interfere, responding instead of our guest. "And then Sergio is a chef, so I would make a bad figure if I cooked for him..."

I must try to save myself from this situation that seems to be without escape.

"Come on!" Andrea esclaims. "You are a chef? This point Rebbi did not tell me."

Again? So he really decided to put his safety at risk tonight!

"S T O P I T!", I say with the labial, so that only

he who is watching me can understand.

"Well, she really only discovered it tonight" Sergio clears up. "Anyway I thank you for the invitation but I have to go, also because Barney will surely need to take a walk."

Luckily!

I could not have sustained all this pressure for a long time

"Thank you again Sergio" I repeat once again accompanying him to the door.

"You do not have to keep thanking me."

"Yes, yes. I would not have known what to do."

"Good night Rebecca" he whispers, and without me being able to foresee it, he gives me a kiss on my cheek, catching me completely unprepared, so that in moving our lips almost touch.

OH, - FOR - THE - MISERY!

I think I could still fall on his feet right now, and I certainly do not want it to happen a second time in the same evening!

"Good night to you too", I answer with a faint voice.

I close the door and finally, after two hours, I go back to breathing normally.

"Why you did not stay at Marco's house tonight?" I ask Andrea pretending to be angry.

"Because he has to get up very early tomorrow morning, so he basically kicked me out! He says that when we sleep together, he wakes up more tired. I just can not understand why!"

"Right, not even me. You're always the same!" I burst out laughing. "But I am glad to have you all for me tonight, despite your behaviour of a little ago."

"I just wanted to help you."

"And what did you do before, you would call it help? As if the situation had not already been sufficiently disastrous."

"Someone must take the first step, and since you do not decide..." he insists.

"Forget it!" I exclaimed exasperated, and I begin to tell him everything that happened between me and Sergio, until the time of his arrival.

"I can not believe you did not take advantage of the situation!" Andrea exclaims almost scandalized, as soon as I finish talking. "Apparently you need a little revise..."

"Stop it Andy! After all, if you analyze things well, you can say that I do not even him."

"Indeed! It would have been the right time to deepen the knowledge, don't think so? Instead you have thought well to make it go away on the most beautiful moment!"

"Nothing would have happened between us anyway" I reaffirm convinced. "For all I know he could also be engaged."

"You said the right word: he could be!"

"I don't know Andy, I feel confused. And then I told him too many lies..."

"Why did not you tell him the truth now that you had the chance? What do you think he cares about how you used to be at that time?" he scolds me.

"Perhaps he could not not care about it, as you say, but I do care!" I esclaims. "And anyway, after what has happened with Giulio, I do not intend to suffer again for a men." On this I am firmly convinced.

"In my opinion you should simply let yourself go. After all, what do have to lose?"

Maybe nothing, he is right.

"So you think I should just throw in another relationship, even if I risk crashing again?"

I do not know why I asked for it since I already know your answer.

"The only risk you could run is to be happy again" he answers me, just as I imagined.

"I do not even know if I am his type", I continue then, following the trail of my chronic pessimism.

"Surely you will never know if you continue to remain closed between these four walls. You have to give him, and also to yourself, a second chance."

"I will reflect about it."

"You think too much."

"I know" I admit.

I sit on the couch next to him and lean my head

on his shoulder. "What would I do without you?"

"You would spend a sad, lonely and monotonous life."

"Long live the sincerity!"

"We order a pizza?"

"Pizza would be! I was a bit hungry with all this thinking…"

15

Become very late.

Andrea has already gone to sleep for a while. I instead remain sitting on the couch staring at the emptiness.

I do not want to go to bed because I'm afraid I can not get to sleep that easily. Then, driven by an inexplicable impulse, I go into my room and open the closet drawer where I keep some old photographs, locked in a wooden box.

I lie down on my stomach, open the box and start looking at them one by one.

My parents are portrayed in one of the many. They smile, looking into each other's eyes and holding hands. In the background Piazza San Marco during their honeymoon in Venice.

They are young, have a lifetime ahead, and above

all they are very much in love. They love each other of that pure and innocent love that everyone hopes to experience at least once in their life, and that resists time, after more than thirty years of marriage. Despite the countless problems of everyday life, economic insecurities, the fear of not being able to raise two daughters, and that their love is not enough, they are still together, today as then.

I always feel a strong emotion in looking at this image, and a tear looks shy in my eyes.

In other photos I see myself and my sister as children.

Some shots are really very funny and make me smile. In one of these I am three years old, with my face all dirty with sauce while I eat a plate of spaghetti, or in another with my father's hat lowered on the forehead, far too large for my head so small.

Then there is Ottavia on her first day of kindergarten, with blonde hair and her round and red cheeks. And then the two of us together that we play at the park, while we push on the swing, or while we make our snowman a little 'disproportionate; and then to the sea, completely submerged by the sand.

How many memories, one more wonderful than the other, when everything in life seemed to me easy, attainable and possible. Exactly the opposite of now.

I keep my old secret diary under these dozens of photographs.

In fact, more than a diary is a real brick, since over time, finishing each time the space to write, I have combined more than one. Only the cover has always remained the original one.

I take it in my hands and I run the pages up to the first, then I begin to read it, inevitably losing myself between its strictly written lines with the blue ballpoint...

21 May 1998

Dear Diary,
I am Rebecca.
Today I am thirteen years old and I am very happy, because I will finally have a trusted friend to whom I can tell everything about me, without hiding anything...

... now, unfortunately, I have to leave you. I have to study math because for sure tomorrow the prof. will questions me, and I already have a good four to recover....
See you soon!

22 May 1998

Dear Diary,
This morning at school was disgusting!
I took another five in the query.
I HATE MATHEMATIC!
And then, like it was not enough, that stupid of Elisa (I HATE HER TOO!) she started playing dumb with Luca!
It's not right!
It's from elementary school that I have a crush on him, even though I've never had the courage to point it out.
But how do the other girls brings down all the boys at their feet?
I will never be like one of them...

The time in effects has agreed with me...

30 May 1999

Dear Diary,
in a few days the school will end and I will have to take the eighth grade exams.
I'm already very tense and I just hope everything ends as soon as possible and in the best way.
But will I be sufficiently prepared?

128

How I wish my problems today were still school exams...

8 September 1999

Hi Diary,
tomorrow for me will be the first day of high school.

It still does not seem true to me!

I am excited and also quite terrified at the thought.

It will undoubtedly be a nice change. New teachers, new classmates and new subjects to study. I hope to live up to it, and above all to be able to make new friends...

It makes a strange effect to re-read these pages, and I have the feeling of having written them only a short time ago, but many years have passed since then.

After all, however, in spite of the time that flows, I have not changed much since then, so much so that in every single word I can still recognize myself: a little girl - now that become a woman - sensitive and too insecure, full of uncertainties and fragilities, who wants to know the world, but who unfortunately is afraid to explore it.

16 November 2005

Dear Diary,

I have a shocking new: today I have known a boy!

His name is Giulio and he attends the same faculty. He is really nice, apart from being funny and very easy.

He invited me to go out with him, and I accepted.

I still can not believe it of having done that!

I've never gone out with a guy before, and I'm electrified to say the least.

What if he finds me boring? Or worse yet, try to kiss me?

But above all: how should you behave on a first date?

Of course I was really a mass!

Not that now it is particularly improved in fact.

However, I still remember very well my first date with Giulio...

19 November 2005

Hi Diary,

this evening I went out with Giulio, and him as I was afraid (but maybe within myself I hope), he tried to kiss me!

My initial reaction was total PANIC!

Although Giulio was immediately a true gentleman, I was afraid of being judged, since I never kiss anyone before, and between theory and practive there is really a great difference!

If I think back to that evening I am smiling, then I continue to leaf through the pages of the diary and the bad memories assail me once again.

21 May 2015

Dear Diary,

today is my thirtieth birthday, pity only I have no desire to celebrate.

Today I find nothing that is worthwhile to be happy.

In a week I should have married.

I should have... But Giulio decided to cancel everything definitively, just like the sign of a pencil made by mistake on a piece of paper.

And perhaps this was our relationship for him in all these years: only one terrible mistake.

30 May 2015

Hi Diary,

I'm in pieces and I can not find the strength to overcome this ugly moment.

I feel destroyed and full of anger, and I can not avoid wondering why all this happened to me.

For ten years I was happy, I felt loved, protected and desired.

Now instead I am back to the starting point, and I feel fragile, just like at that time.

Maybe there's really something wrong with me...

Some memories always leave a bitter taste in my mouth, and are so oppressive as to make me feel overwhelmed by their weight.

I should try to get rid of it, because I know that sooner or later they will end up crushing me and getting the better of me.

Instinctively I tear off the last pages and I do

them in dozens of very small pieces, just like my heart has been torn apart.

It would be good to be able to eliminate even unpleasant memories, and I know that I should throw some of these behind and start to finally look forward, but this is unfortunately not as easy as tearing up a sheet.

The only thing I want now is to find the courage to turn the page of my life.

But will I really be able to do it

16

It's eight thirty, and to wake me up suddenly is the ringtone of my cell phone.

I'm sure it's Cinzia and she wants to know how it went yesterday between Barney and my Honey.

"Hi Cinzia", I answer still sleepy and with a slightly kneaded voice.

"Good Morning Rebbi, I hope I did not wake you up."

"Don't worry. Among other things, I think I also forgot to put the alarm clock last night..."

With all that has happened, it seems to me the least!

"So, all fine?" she is asking me right away. "I saw Sergio in passing this morning, but as usual he is always in a hurry and I could not ask him much."

"It went very well. Your brother really helped me a lot" I say sincerely.

"I told you. He knows what to do. And then?"

And then what? What else she wants me to tell her?

"Then we chatted about this and that, and then he went away with Barney."

For obvious reasons I omit the details of the flight of the tray and my poor performance.

"Well, I am glad that there is harmony between you, since you will meet often."

Yes sure. Maybe before I spilled two glasses of tea on him!

"Right…" I say embarrassed in the memory of the episode, and also because of its affirmation.

The fact that Sergio and I will be forced to see us frequently continues to not exite me at all.

"I am happy that he distracted himself a bit…" Cinzia continues.

"What do you mean?" I ask curiously.

"Well, I do not know if my brother told you about it, actually knowing it I do not think he did. Anyway, I meant distracted by the thought of that harpy of his girlfriend. She is driving him crazy!"

I knew it! He has a girlfriend!

This time Andrea's sixth sense has failed. But the awareness of being right about it does not make me happy at all.

"Sergio is engaged?" I ask hesitantly, perhaps still hoping to have misunderstood, and that she can answer no, even though it seems obvious to me now that the opposite.

"Ex girlfriend, actually. They have just left each other" she answer. "Sergio has finally decided to drop her, but that witch does not want to leave him in peace, and continues to harass him."

Maybe Andrea was not completely wrong then, and deep down I'm already sprinkling joy from all the pores.

"Sergio did not tell me anything" I confirm, "and from how you talk about it, I understand that this person is not to your liking."

"In fact it is so. She was staying with my brother only for her personal gain. I had guessed it from the beginning."

The instinct of a sister is hardly mistaken. The same thing happens between me and Ottavia.

"I understand" I only say.

"Instead Sergio has never managed to realize it, until now."

I almost do not believe my ears: Sergio in love, and moreover of a girl who was with him only out of interest!

Then there is a divine justice to this world!

"I am sorry" I say to be polite, even if it is not exactly what I think. After all, the fact that he too could have suffered for love, gives me a bit of satisfaction for all that I have also passed because of him.

"You could be his type, you know?" Cinzia asks me in a retoric manner, interrupting the course of my thoughts.

I understood well?

Maybe Cinzia doesn't know so much her brother as she believes.

"I don't think so...", but I do not end my sentence. "For when did you plan your departure?" I ask her to change subject.

"Next week" she answer. "Meantime I would like to bring you to see my new house, so that at least you can have an idea."

"Agree."

"Perfect. I call you in these days."

I close the conversation with Cinzia, I do a light breakfast, I put on a jumper and tennis shoes and I go out.

Running makes me feel good, but I continue to have the pounding thought of Sergio in mind. And then I was troubled by what his sister told me, not so much because of his ex, as for the idea that I could be his type. It seems unlikely to say the least, although he has changed considerably.

I try to imagine how this girl looks like. For sure she will be beautiful and attractive, but apparently not at all worthy of being by his side, and I feel a bit guilty for what I thought a moment ago. In the end he will also have been a perfect asshole in high school, but for this it certainly does not deserve to have an anchor as a girlfriend.

I stop a few minutes on a bench to catch my breath.

My eyes are half closed, and I am completely lost in my thoughts that I do not perceive anything of what is around me.

"Ciao Rebecca", I hear suddently.

I open my eyes wide and jump into the air with fright. Then I turned my head and I realized that he is the boy of the other morning, and that moreover his dog has just nestled on my feet.

Again him?

"Sorry. It was not my intention to scare you" he says.

I believe it!

"For this time I will survive."

"Well, I could always help you if you felt bad. I must admit that I would not be sorry at all..."

Now also try to do the brilliant? But why do not you leave me alone?

I just want to relax. Alone. FIVE MINUTES!

"Thank you, but I would prefer not to be help by

anyone."

"I can imagine… Where is your dog?" he asks me.

"Is not my dog, I told you already. I take care of him only when his mistress is not there" I answer more and more annoyed.

"Forgive me, I did not want to bother you. It is clear that you want to be alone."

Finally!

"See you next time", he says standing up.

"Wait" I stop him. "You can seat down, and pardon me" I came back on myself.

"You really are a nice person do you know? You're nice anyway, as well as very pretty."

"Are you always so full of compliments?"

"Beside being quite irritating?", I wanted to add.

"Not always. Only when I meet a girl like you."

"What you want to say with *a "girl like you"*?"

"Well, I believe you know perfectly how you are, and therefore what I mean…" he alluds.

"If this also wanted to be a flattering thank you, even if the compliments actually gives me of embarrassment."

"I thought so…"

But who is he, a sensitive maybe?

"And from what would you have understood that, if it is right to know?"

"From how you place yourself towards others" he answers. "You always seem to be on the defensive."

"You are wrong. It is not."

But how does he take this liberty? He does not even know me!

I did wrong to make him stay.

"Don't take it. Mine did not want to be an offence."

"I do not doubt it, even if it did look like one. Anyway maybe it is true…" I admit with a certain difficulty.

"You struggle to trust people, and you'll probably have your own good reasons, but you have to learn to let go. Being closed in on yourself is not always good."

"You will not be a brainshrink?" I ironically ask.

"Absolutely not" he answer laughing.

I notice once again that when he smiles he really has beautiful features, even if it is not exactly my ideal of man.

Not very tall, he still has a nice body. Red hair, light eyes, and some freckles spread on the face.

"Sorry" I tell him suddenly, "but I think I really do not remember your name" I confess with a mortified air.

"Then I will not tell you" he states. "In this way you are forced to think of me to be able to remember it."

This guy is really a weird guy, and also very cheeky.

Do you really think you're that important?

I have other thoughts on my mind that do not

bother about his identity!

"See you Rebecca" he says standing up.

"See you" I answer, just to be gentle, but I really hope that I will not have to meet him every time I come to run to the park.

I'm still sitting on the bench and I've just received a message from an unknown number.
Who will be now?

Hi Rebecca, how are you? I read.
I'm Sergio.

Of course I do not have a moment of relax!

I allowed myself to ask for your number to my sister, I continue to read. *I hope you do not mind.*
I would like to see you again, so what would you say about an invitation at dinner?
Have a good day and see you soon.

He asked for my number to Cinzia and is inviting me to dinner? I can not believe it!

At this point I should answer, even if I do not know exactly what.

Hello Sergio. I'm glad you asked for my number

NO!

Definitely so it can not go.

In this way it almost seems that I was not waiting for anything but his invitation!

Cancel and rewrite.

Hello Sergio. I do not mind that your sister gave you my number.

Me too would like to see you one of these days…

We are not!

I erase once again.

Hello Sergio. It's not a problem if Cinzia gave you my number.

As for the invitation, I'm sorry, but I do not think it's possible. I'm already busy, I reply vague, without letting him understand the real motivation of my refusal.

I just hope he does not insist. I do not think it would be a good idea to go out with him. So I press the ENTER key, before I can think again, and I stare at the phone for a few minutes, waiting for an answer.

Okay then, when you wish, he writes.

See you soon Rebecca.

"Possibly NEVER!", but it is obvious that I can not write it to him.

See you soon, I simply reply.

I am still doubtful about his first message, and I am forced to reread it over and over again before realizing that it is not just the fruit of my imagination.

Sergio really asked me for an appointment!

Is it possible for a boy like him to be interested in someone like me?

Despite the circumstances, this awareness can only leave me flattered and awaken my dormant female pride in me, if I ever had it!

Giulio was my first and only boyfriend, so it is inevitable that all this sudden attention from another man leaves me completely confused and even a bit dazed. Not to mention the fact that only the idea of going out with another person, and of having the second *first date* of my life, provokes me not a little disquiet.

17

I've been in the Polytechnic library for a couple of hours, where I usually stop to study after class. Here I can concentrate better, surrounded by books and the sad buzz of people.

It's November, and I'm in my first year of study at the Faculty of *Design and Arts*.

I moved to Milan for less than two months. I do

not know anyone yet and my introverted character is certainly not helping me to make new friends.

My cousin Sara continues to invite me out, but I decline every time, with the excuse of always having something to do.

At the beginning of September I went to live with my aunt Anna, my mother's sister. Her daughter is my same age and attends the course of literature and philosophy at the Statale. She was immediately very happy with my move to her home. Being an only child, after the separation of my aunt by her ex-husband when she was only ten years old, she has always suffered a little solitude, despite having a very expansive and extrovert character.

When I enrolled at university, I initially planned to commute, although obviously it would have been much more stressful and difficult. But when my aunt had known that I would attend the faculty in Milan, she did not want to hear reasons, and had welcomed me to her house with open arms.

So now I go back to Pavia only every two or three weeks to spend the weekend with my parents.

Today the program of the day is identical to that of all other days: four hours of lessons, a sandwich on the fly and then total immersion on the study until late afternoon. As long as I can, I want to try not to fall behind with the exams.

I am trying to tidy up my notes on the history of

art, which unfortunately are a bit messed up since the prof. he's talking too fluent, but something distracts me.

I noticed that the guy sitting on the other side of the table has been watching me for some time. He smiles at me, and I do not know what else to do with embarrassed spare, immediately averting my gaze. But a second later I find him sitting next to me.

"Hi" he greats me.

"Hi" I respond with no care and also visibly annoyed.

"My name is Giulio. We have already seen each other at the lesson. Remember?"

"Uhm uhm..." I answer, continuing to keep my eyes on the book.

"I wanted to ask you, without turning around too much, if by chance you would go out with me one of these days."

Did I get it right? This guy I do not even know has just asked me to go out with him?

"I don't think I have time", I answer a little bitgarly.

"I promise I will not steal you more than a couple of hours, just long enough to take you for a drink. Come on, do not make people pray you..."

At this point I raise my head and look at him seriously irritated.

It's really cute, and I've certainly never noticed it before, perhaps because I tend to never observe anyone. After all, no one has ever even noticed me!

"I repeat that this is not the case. And then I do not even know you", I replied convinced.

"Of course you know me. I just told you my name", he insists. "By the way, what's yours?"

What a kind of nonsense!

"Can you explain to me why you would like to go out with a girl whose identity you do not even know?"

"Simple, because it was enough for me to cross your gaze once, to understand that I can not do without it."

Wow!

Sentence a bit obvious, but certainly effective. And as incurable as they are romantic, this is enough to make me give in.

I woke up early and inexplicably in a good mood this morning, and taken by this moment of positive charge I even decided to go to the hairdresser.

It's an eternity that Michi - the hairdresser in question, precisely -, does not see in my face.

I called to his salon very early (not wanting to risk having to wait forever!), and luckily I managed to get an appointment in the early afternoon, otherwise in the meantime I would almost certainly have changed my mind.

The crazy hands I like it very much, even if due to my semi-depression of the recent months I have not been there for a long time. I took care of its furniture when it opened a few years ago, and it was also my first real paid job.

I put all my efforts into its realization, creating as usual a welcoming and relaxing environment, but at the same time modern and fresh, with a certain chic and original tone.

Michi had greatly appreciated my work, proving immediately enthusiasm about the result, so much so that in the end between us two was even born a beautiful friendship. It was him who should have styled my hair on my wedding day, and when he had known that Giulio had left me, his reaction had been a mixture of regret for me and anger towards him.

"Dear Rebbi, finally! It's nice to see you again", he came to me as soon as he sees me to great me.

"It's nice also for me to back here" I say, while we hold each other in a sincere hug.

"How are you?" he asks me. "You really deserve a real earshot. It's months that you don't make yourself alive!"

"You are right. But in the last period I have not particularly taken care of myself...", I answer in a sorry voice. "I just hope that is not noticeable too much!" In fact, during all this time my hair has become more indomitable than usual.

"I'll take care of it now. For your hair I can definitely do something, for the rest..." interrupted himself, perhaps due to the fear of investigating my current sentimental situation.

"Nothing has changed since the last time we talk together. I'm still alone, if that's what you want to know. But I'm trying to make a change in my life, and I came to you for this too!" I affirm with conviction.

"I'm glad to hear you talking like that. Are you sure that a man is not involved in this change?"

My mind immediately runs to Sergio, but immediately I try to keep myself from thinking about him.

"To be honest, no. I want to come back from the abyss in which I fell, and I want to do it only for myself."

"This is the Rebecca I know! Come on, loosen this kind of tail, so that I can see the extent of the damage!" he says, winking at me.

I fulfill his request and remove the rubber band that keeps them tied, but from his expression I immediately realize that the situation is worse than I thought.

"Oh, my goodness! There will be a lot to work here!" he exclaims with an expression almost terrified. "Bea come and prepare Misses Rebecca."

I do not know this Bea. It must be the last girl assumed by Michi, and this makes me really understand how long I have been missing from here, and also how much I isolated myself from everything and everyone.

The new helper seems little more than a girl and has a cheeky look, obviously very suitable for her young age. She has a nose piercing and I believe at least two or three more for each ear; hair brush with colorful locks ranging from bright red to fuchsia, and a trick to say the least flashy.

I look at her, feeling a little envy. In spite of everything it would be nice to be able to still have her age.

"I could do my hair like hers", I tell him this jocking and indicating her. "What do you think Michi? I would certainly demonstrate at least ten years less."

"Yes sure, so you would be absolutely perfect to enter the club of morrons!"

We both burst out laughing.

"Ok, received. I put myself in your hands. Make me what you want, without exaggerating too much I recommend. I would like to recognize myself in the mirror again when I leave your saloon."

"If you do not stop it right away, I'll get you out of here with green and blue hair!" he threatens me in response, immidiately putting himself to work.

When Michi finishes his work, more than two hours have passed, and my appearance is completely renewed.

This was exactly what I wanted, even if the first

impact was almost a shock. But I have to admit that the more I look at myself in the mirror, the happier I am of the excellent result.

Michi has revolutionized my original color, making me pass from a dark and dull chestnut to a lighter one with coppery reflections; but above all from an indefinite and harmonyless cut to a climbed with fringe, which highlights the outline of my face.

Basically unrecognizable!

I decide to take a selfie, which normally I would never give my total repulsion to photograph me, and send it to Andrea. I'm sure that seeing it will be as shocked as I am.

For some time he had been begging me to change my look, and I must admit that I should have listened to him much earlier, because my trusted coiffeur really surpassed himself and my expectations.

Before going to take Barney I jumped home to change. When I'm about to leave, I get a message from Cinzia.

Hi Rebecca.
Would you like to meet us later? she asks me.
I'll take you to see the villa if you do not have any other plans.

No programs. Send me the address, see you there.

As I wait for her answer, I call Andrea.

"Hi shine. Who are you?" he immidiately attacks. "Do we know each other maybe? One thing is certain: if I were heterosexual I would like to meet you!"

"But how stupid you are!" I say laughing. "However, from your appreciation I assume that my new style is to your liking."

"Jocking? Of course! You are a charm."

"Thanks Andy, you were right. I already feel another, and it took only a very simple hairstyle."

"Remember that I am always right."

"Now don't exagerate!" I admonish him. "See you this evening?"

"Yes sure. See you later."

I'm happy with how things are going in the last days. If only it were not for Sergio…

His sudden break from the past in my present was not foreseen, and I still can not decide whether I like it or not. I still feel mixed feelings towards him, a mixture of curiosity and attraction for the man who has become, but also of anger and frustration for the boy who was and for what made me suffer, even if in an unconscious manner.

I do not know if I'll ever have the courage to tell him the truth. Sometimes I wish old Rebecca had never existed, and especially that he never remembered her.

18

The new home of Cinzia is located in a newly built area, in a complex of houses surrounded by greenery.

I imagine that to be able to afford to come to live in a context like this, you have to earn quite well with your work, or have rather wealthy and quite generous parents!

I park my car at number two, right in front of her house. I play a couple of times on the intercom and the gate opens onto the avenue of the garden, which is nothing short of huge and surrounds the whole house. I think it's at least as big as my whole apartment!

The facade of the villa is in sight, a detail that gives it an absolutely delightful appearance.

As I walk down the path, one comes to mind detail: outside I did not notice the car of Cinzia parked, and I do not know for what strange reason but I immediately have a very bad presentiment, which obviously can not remain just such.

"Hi Rebecca" Sergio greeted me in fact opening the door and looking at me for a long time.

Sure: the new hairstyle!

"Hi Sergio. I had an appointment with your sister..."

If this is a trap designed by her, I have no intention of falling in it!

Now I turn around and go away instantly!

"That's why I am here" he is saying. "Cinzia had an unexpected event at the last minute and could not warn you. So she asked me to make you visit the house.”

An unexpected event? I do not know if I believe…

“She could also call me and we could have postpone the apointment!” I say altered within myself, but evidently not in a tone quite subdued not to be heard, in fact Sergio asks me immediately: “Does it bother you that I am here instead of her?”

“Of course not!” I try to recover from the gaffe. “I am just wondering why she did not warn me” I answer all red in my face.

“Do you want to visit the house or do you think you will stay on the threshold for a long time?” he asks me in a singing type of tone.

This episode seems to me like a déjà-vu!

“Of course, sorry…” I say hesitating. “I brought the camera with me.”

“Ok, go ahead…”

“You thought you were a super busy person. It amazes me that you have found the time to be here.” I say to soften a bit my embarassement.

“I am a man of a thousand resources! Anyway, this new hairstyle fits you very well”, he make his compliments, continuing to stare at me.

“Thank you” I say only this, while obviously I get red even more.

I hate my reaction to embarrassment, especially because the awareness of becoming bordeaux colored in difficult situations, provokes me even more insecurity, further worsening my state

Exactly like a cat biting his own tale!

Sergio precedes me by a step, and I follow him tracing sketches with a pencil on a sheet; but I'm distracted, so without realizing it I'm going to end up on him, stomping his foot.

Our faces are very close and our lips almost touch, for the second time.

"Sorry" I say trying to get myself back.

"Of nothing."

"This house is really very nice and very bright. I like it."

I would like to see! Who would not like it?

"Cinzia did a great deal buying it. Think that the old owner has sold it to a tattered price" he explain me. "I think he was in a hurry to sell because of an imminent transfer abroad."

"So she was really very lucky then. A house like this is an excellent investment" I say like I was an expert. "Will you also come to live here too?" I inform myself, even if I remember he had already mentioned it.

I do not understand why I still do not do my business!

"Initially yes" he answer. "Then I'll start looking for something on my own. My sister and I are very close, but we can not live long under the same roof. We have characters that are too different, and for this we often clash."

"I understand you. Also me and my sister are

very different" I say smaling, thinking about Ottavia. "But she live with my parents, and I believe she does not intend to leave very soon."

"And you instead? Have you been living with that *roommate* for a long time?"

I note like he puts a particular emphasis on the last word, almost as if doubting the fact that between me and Andrea there is only a bond of friendship.

"Since a few months" I answer, ignoring the reasons why. "I could never live alone. But since the cohabitation with my mother has never been exactly peaceful, I preferred to have my independence soon enough."

"For me it's all the same, even if more than anything else I do not get along with the person who calls himself "my father"."

"Your relationship is so bad?" I still investigate, since the momeny that already last time he gave the reason to think of that.

"It is" he answer. Then he adds: "Several years ago he drop me and my family from one day to another, without any precise explanation, disappearing in the nowhere. Per what I know he got himself transferred to Paris" he tells.

He observe the emptyness while he speaks. It is evident that this sad chapter of his life makes him still feel very bad.

"It's been fifteen years since then" he carries on.

"When he showed up again, after a long time, I did not want anything to do with."

"I am sorry" I sinceraly say, because I can only imagine how difficult it could have been for him, and also for Cinzia, to grow up without a father figurr at his side.

"When he came back he wanted to re-establish relations with me and my sister. He called us and looked for us all the time. Until one year ago he did not return to our home, as if nothing had happened. But the worst thing is that our mother has allowed it", he sighs and stops talking for a few minutes, which seems eternal to me. I feel powerless in the face of his uneasiness that I can not alleviate.

"During all the years spent in his absence, my mother has never stopped loving him, despite all that she suffered for his cause" he takes back telling. "I was furious, and still I can not accept living under the same roof as an individual that I can barely call father."

Listening to his outburst in silence, finding some similarities between me and Sergio's mother. Even I, like her, had been left overnight, without a logical explanation; I too had initially hoped that Giulio would return, because I did not think I could live without him. Now, however, things appear to me very different: if Giulio were to live again at this moment, he would receive what he deserves.

I could never forgive him.

"I apologize, I should not have asked you", it's the only thing I can say when I finally find the courage to speak.

"It's me that I should apologize for making you a part of this."

"Not at all. And anyway it's good that you can talk about it."

"I do not know why, but it's as if you and I have known each other for a long time..."

His spontaneity is disarming.

"How did Cinzia react to his return?" I ask him, trying to ignore his words.

"Fortunately, my sister has a strong character, and certainly has faced the situation better than me" he admits. "Our father has always missed her so much, while I believe I have never really felt his absence; I was too angry to even notice it."

"You had all the right."

"Do you know what the funny thing is?" he question with a fake smile. "After he left us, he continued to send us expensive presents. The money for him was never a problem, and perhaps he thought in this way of being able to buy our love too."

"Or maybe he was just trying to make up for it" I hypothesize.

"Maybe, but it did not work with me. On the contrary, he got the exact opposite" he says harshly. "Do you remember when I told you about me as a teenager?"

"Yes" I answer. I remember it all right!

"Growing up I realized that my arrogant and presumptuous behavior was used only to vent the rancor I felt towards him" he explains. "I went on for so long, until I realized that I had to use that rage in a positive way and commit myself to realize something concrete for myself. In this way I managed to get my revenge."

Listening to his words, many aspects of his character and what he has been in the past appear to me much clearer. I wish I could tell him that now I finally understand the reasons for his attitude, and that I could probably also forgive him, but I can not do it.

Suddenly I realize that we have been talking for more than half an hour, and that moreover he showed me only a small part of the villa.

"It will be better to continue" I say hurriedly, interrupting that moment of intimacy that had been created between us until a moment before.

"You are right" Sergio confirms, but in a fraction of a second he takes my hand, drawing me to himself, and puts a light kiss on my lips.

I remain still, eyes wide in amazement.

I would like to reciprocate with all of myself, but the memory of his words ten years ago resurfaces forcefully in my head.

"I could never kiss a girl like that…"

I can not even move a muscle. My mind is rebelling against this unexpected contact, so terribly warm and soft, but my body does not want to know how to do the same, so I give up, not being able to do anything else than let myself go.

Sergio perceives having knocked down the wall of my initial reticence and attracts me even more to himself, hugging me tightly in his arms.

I would like this kiss to last forever, but the still ratiocinating part of my brain immediately regains control, and makes my lips move away from his.

"It's since I met you that I want to do it", Sergio whispers to me.

"You should not have done it!", I would like to shout, but these words remain only a muffled scream.

"You don't know anthing about me." My tone is abrupt in trying to move him away.

"Your eyes tell me Rebecca, and they tell me everything I want to know. You can not hide anything until I will be allowed to look at them."

He is not talking seriously!

Curse of my treacherous eyes! They always revealed too much of me.

"I… I am already engaged, I am sorry" I prounance without reflecting, reading the disappointment on his face.

I feel guilty for this umpteenth and shameless lie, but I can not blame myself. After all he had always despised me. And then he probably even recognized me, and he just having fun making a fool of me.

But could it really get to that? Not the guy who sits in front of me. Or at least I think.

Sergio really looks like another person, but I do not know if I would have the courage to risk and try his change on my skin. I am too afraid of suffering again, and after all my heart has not yet completely recovered from the last wound that has been inflicted on it.

This situation has now eluded me, and I see no solution to get out unscathed. Whatever I can do or say, it would surely be the wrong one.

I do not like to lie, but now I'm in it up to my neck.

Sergio no longer said a word, while I continued to take pictures, take notes and make sketches.

"Well, I think I have all the material I need" I say at some point, dissolving for a moment the tension created between us.

Thanks God I can finally leave from here.

"Rebecca, what happened just a moment ago..." he blocks himself. His disturbance is almost palpable.

"It does not matter, do not worry" I interrupt him.

Better not to get lost in further explanations.

"I'll take you back to the door."

"I know the way, thanks" I say without even looking him.

I walk down the avenue to the gate, feeling his gaze settle on my back, but I do not turn around.

I could even be so crazy to go back.

I get in the car and take a deep breath.

I still can not realize what has just happened, and the set of emotions felt by the contact of his lips laid on mine is indescribable.

How long had I wanted that kiss once?

I have dreamed so many of those times, that now it seems impossible that it could have really happened.

19

Sergio is kissing me and I spare him with passion.

I do not know where we are or how long we've been here, and anyway I do not care. The only thing I want is to be able to stay that way, lost in our mutual embrace, with no more lies, no bad memories. There are only us two, in our present.

But suddenly he looks at me and turns away disgusted. He tells me I'm horrible, and I'm not at his height. Then he starts laughing.

"Did you really believe that I could fall in love with someone like you? You're just a stupid girl Rebecca!", and continues to laugh louder and louder.

I wake up with a start. I must have fallen asleep while watching TV sitting on the couch. It is one o'clock at night, and my worst nightmare has just emerged from the past.

I would not have had to go to the appointment with Cinzia this afternoon, indeed to tell the truth I would not even have to respond to your announcement!

By this time I would not have met Sergio, he would not have kissed me, and my ghosts would not have come back to torment me!

But how could I even imagine that this could

have happened?

Probably someone, somewhere, will surely be wrong to shuffle the cards of my destiny!

I have no intention of falling in love again, and moreover of Sergio. I no longer want to allow anyone to make me suffer, let alone him.

I get up from the sofa to go to bed and hear the sound of the key turning in the lock. Fortunately, Andrea has returned home.

"Hi dear. Is it all fine?" he asks me, as if looking at me as soon as he has already guessed my state of mind.

"Yes" chin, although I know perfectly well that with him it is useless.

"You would not say" in fact he tells me, looking at me in the face. "What happened? You have a face!"

"What do you want me to have at this time of night?" I reply to try to misguide your question.

"You do not tell it to me. You are the reflection of depression! Come on, spit the toad" insists.

Of course I can not bear his head, so I tell him everything that happened in the afternoon, without leaving out any detail.

"I believe that you are making too much problems" he tells me when I finished to talk.

"Maybe it will be like that too. However you know that right now I do not want to have a new relationship. It's too early, and I do not feel ready yet."

"You are wrong Rebbi, and you know it" he repreminds me.

"Even if it were, it's too late now. I told him a lot of lies. Even that of being engaged!"

Andrea looks at me with obvious disapproval.

"I really can not understand you. Why are you trying in every way to complicate your existence?"

"I am just trying to defend myself", I firmly reply.

"Do you think you should continue to defend yourself forever? And from what then?"

Is useless. Even he can not understands me.

"Can we close this thread? It does not really matter now, since I can not go back."

"There is always a way to go back, just want it."

"Do you want to stop from always being so pedantic? You are really exasperating!" And for the first time in all these years I think it seriously.

20

Today it seems to be a really beautiful day, even though it's already October and the time of year is approaching that I love less.

Fortunately, despite the very bad prospect of last night, I managed to sleep peacefully without nightmares this night. But of course, as soon as I opened my eyes, my first thought could not be anyone but Sergio.

I can not stop fantasizing about our kiss, and instinctively I pass the tip of my tongue over my lips, as if to still want to taste its essence, astonishing myself of my gesture.

Andrea is already out of the house, early in the morning as always (at least he could not resume tormenting me!), and I decide to go running.

Cinzia asked me to take Barney to the vet this afternoon, since she is still very busy with the preparations for her imminent departure.

No problem, I had answered the phone.

"Apart from the fact that I would like to make sure I do not find your brother again!" I would have

166

gladly added.

The fear of meeting him does not make me feel comfortable, and I go to Cinzia's house, full of concern.

Barney, as soon as he sees me, lets himself go into a profusion of parties.

"Hi beauty! I missed you" I say him accaressing him, but immediately he begins to sneeze repeatedly, even looking very agitated.

"But what does he have?" I ask.

"I don't know. It's been like that since yesterday. Maybe he just have a cold" Cinzia replies.

Sergio, thanks God, does not seems to be around. This time I escaped!

"The vet, unfortunately, is a bit out of the way", she explains me. "About three quarters of an hour by car."

"Ok. I will settle the navigator" I say, since I would be able to lose myself even a few steps from home!

"I do not know him in person" she specifies. "It was raccomended to me by a friend. This is the address" she says handing me over his business card. "The appointment is at 15:00."

"Perfect. We will be very punctual."

"I apologize for yesterday" adds changing the subject, "but I had a held up in the last minute."

"Don't worry."

But next time warn!

"Also start throwing down some ideas and then
send me everything via email. When I return I will
define the various details better."

"Agree."

"I am sure you will do a great job" she says
seriously.

I smile back.

The trust she places on my abilities makes me
proud of myself, and I am very grateful for that.

The vet is in a village unknown to me, so given
my innate ability to lose myself, I asked Ottavia to
accompany me.

We are in the car since more than half and hour,
and the navigator indicates 10 minutes upon arrival
at the destination. But suddenly I hear a stange
noise coming from outside, ike something attached
to the rim of the car that keeps rattling against it.

I immidiately have a bad feeling.

"Do you hear this ticking too?" I ask to my sister.

She concentrates to listen and then she answer:
"No, I don't hear anything."

I pull the car over and I go down to listen.

The rear wheels seem to be fine to me, so I move
to the front ones. The one on the left seems to me to
be in good condition, but the one on the right is
clearly pierced.

"This one was not needed!"

"What's happening?"

“We got a puncture. And I'm definitely not able to change a tire.”

The only time I had to replace one, Giulio had promptly come to my rescue.

“Don't look at me” Ottavia tells me. “I don't even know from where to begin.”

“We can try at least” I urge her. “Come on, give me a hand. Afterall it would not be so difficult.”

From the bonnet I take out the spare wheel and the jack, and I get to work. However, after a few minutes of testing, I still can't place it under the car to lift it.

But what kind of diabolical contraption is this?

I am already prey to nervousness and frustration, and at this point I seriously begin to hope that someone will stop and give me a hand, since my sister is of no help to me.

“Do you need a helping hand?” asks a voice behind me.

Finally a pious soul!

“Yes, thanks” immediately Ottavia replies instead of me.

“If you would be so kind...” I say. “I really can't place this damn tool!” I scream continuing to fumble, without even turning around.

“In that way I fear you will never succeed.”

“I thinks so too” I have to admit defeat, and I get up to give up our rescuer the place.

“Ciao Rebecca!” this last one esclamais. “But

what an unexpected encounter…”

I raise my head and look at him.

He’s the park boy!

Of all the people who could have stopped, did he have to happen?

“Ciao” I just say, still unable to remember his name.

“Do you know each other?” Ottavia is asking me.

“Right” I reply.

“Very pleased, Lorenzo” he says presenting himself, without taking his eyes away from her.

Lorenzo…

Right!

“Rebbi did not speak to me about you” Ottavia confess, always too frank.

“We met at the park a few days ago…” I vaguely explain.

“What are you doing around here?” he informs himself.

“We were taking Barney to do a check by the vet. We have an appointment in five minutes, and we are damn late!”

“Around here?” he asks.

“Yes” I confirm.

“Is this the case of the Dr Castelli?” he asks again.

“I think is called like that. Do you know him maybe?”

“Only by fame. They say he is very good.”

"Well, we will discover it very soon, or at least I hope so."

"I try to do it as quickly as possible so you do not arrive too" Lorenzo says with the air of someone who knows his stuff. "But rest assured, doctors are never punctual in general."

"And you, why are you here?" I ask at this point, be as well curious.

"I work around here…"

"Really? And where?"

"In a clinic. I am a doctor" he replies fleetingly while he continues to fiddle with various tools.

Lorenzo a doctor? I would never have said it, and it is clear that I have judged it too quickly and superficially, but perhaps in him there is much more than he wants to leave us see.

I watch him fiddle with bolts and wrenches, and imagine him wearing the white coat, while he visits a patient with the same ease. In fact, after a few minutes it has already completed the replacement of the wheel, quickly and efficiently, and I have to admit that without him I would still be on the high seas.

"That's it!" he esclaims. "Now you can go to your appointment."

"Thank you so much. You are great!"

"Of nothing mademoiselle. It is a pleasure to be of use to two beautiful girls like you" he says to both of them, although in reality he seems to be addressing my sister more than anything else, who obviously pretends not to realize the obvious interest he is showing towards her.

"But I seem to remember that the last time we met, you explicitly told me that you would rather not be helped by anyone" specifica poi.

It's true! I said exactly these precise words.

Now instead I find myself having to thank him for helping me.

"We'd better hurry", I say that to not give him satisfaction, turning to Ottavia. "We are definitely late, and I hate making people wait."

"You should take life with more philosophy" Lorenzo replies.

Here we go again!

Here is another of his wisdom pills!

"My sister is uncompromising on some issues to say the least" intervenes Ottavia.

"I noticed" he confirms. "I've already told you once that you should learn to let yourself go."

"I totally agree. If only he wasn't always so stubborn…"

But what is this, a coalition?

"So, do you want to stop to confabulate behind my back?" I ask angrily.

"And why? It's so much fun!" she says.

"Come on, get in the car. We are just losing more time."

Lorenzo gets on his motorbike, give gas and

whizzes away.

"I think you made an impression!" I say to Ottavia to make her angry and take my revenge.

"Stop it, you know very well that is not my type. And then he has the air of one who tries with everyone."

"In fact the first time I saw him he made the same impression on me too" I admit, "but today he was very kind, and maybe I'm changing his mind about him."

"Won't it be that you like him a little bit?" she mischievous hazard.

"Absolutely not!"

We only need Lorenzo, as if I had nothing else to think about.

21

We enter the veterinary clinic, with Barney more and more annoyed with us, and we settle on the armchairs in the waiting room.

Fortunately, despite the delay, we are the only ones waiting, and after a couple of minutes the study door opens, and someone calls Cinzia's name to invite her in.

I seem to know this voice, above all because I am sure it belongs to the same person I spoke to no more than a quarter of an hour ago!

It is probably just my impression, it would be absurd if it were not so. Instead I go into the study and find Lorenzo sitting behind his desk, wearing his white coat.

"You?" I ask incredulously and also a little dazed.

"Well, I told you I am a doctor!" he replies like if nothing happened.

I feel the nervous rise up to the tip of my hair. This person is really annoying!

"You made fun of me! And it's not funny at all!" I

174

exclaim in an exasperated tone.

"Why don't we take care of Barney now? I'll leave you time to insult me later, if you feel like it. And anyway I would like to remind you that you are late, so it is not advisable to do so many sermons."

This is really too much!

"You perfectly know why I am late! And I want to remind you that you are also late!"

"I had an emergency" he tells, making fun of me, while I look at him more and more grimly.

How many vets will there be on the face of earth? It is not possible that Cinzia went to choose him!

Since I met this person, things are happening to me practically one a day!

"Why do I have the distinct feeling that your dog seems much happier than you to see me?" Lorenzo asks me.

"Maybe because I don't love these kind of jokes."

"More lightness Rebecca, this is the cure you need."

"You told me already, less than half and hour ago, and in anycase I am not your patient, my psychologist of my boots!"

"Have you already gone to offenses? And we didn't even arrive on the first date!" he still teases me. "Although, do not hold it against me, but I would much rather go out with Ottavia."

"Listen, let's put immediately things clear: I am here because you, being his vet doctor, you should visit Barney! Therefore could you just do your duty, and stop to flirt?"

If I could I would slap him!

"I see that you remain defensive even when it is not about you."

"Stop with this story! And anyway I would like to remind you that you are talking about my sister, awful Casanova!"

Maybe I'm a little exaggerating, but it's certainly not my fault that this person puts all his efforts into getting me to have a fit!

"I will also be a Casanova, as you say, but why not let her judge this?"

"Don't think about it at all! You tried it with me when we met, admit it!"

"Without offense Rebecca, but you don't reflect my canons, and then Ottavia is much prettier than you!"

He even had the face to tell me this!

"You are really...", the last word dies on my lips. I have to restrain myself, even if with a lot of effort. After all, he's still Barney's vet, and right now we're in his office.

"Carry on" he teases me. "Were you saying?"

I can't stand it, and I wish I could tell him what I think about him.

"I have no intention of responding to your provocations. Why don't you hurry to visit my dog instead?"

"I thought it was not your dog..."

"Infact, you know very well that is not!"

Good havens, he is driving me crazy!

"Your friend here loses her temper too easily" he says whispering, turning to Barney.

I pretend not to hear. I just want to get out of this clinic, hoping to never have to set foot again!

"How long has Barney been sneezing like this and struggling to breathe?" Lorenzo asks me after starting his visit.

"Since yesterday. Why, what does he have?" I ask in alarm.

"Absolutely nothing to worry about. Barney simply inhaled a brome that remained in his nasal cavity."

"What?"

"A spikelet, as it is commonly called."

"Ah..." I still do not understand. "Forgive my ignorance, but how did it stay there?"

"It often happens" says. "Dogs inhale it involuntarily, sniffing in the grass, and it is still in the nose, or worse, it can begin to walk inside it, but this is not the case luckily."

A very professional explanation, there is nothing to say.

"Poor Barney. Who knows what annoyance it must cause him."

"Yes, they are really very annoying" conferms.

"Now I proceed to extract the foreign body and

then check that there is no infection in place."

"Ok" I say turning my back, because I prefer to not assist to this operation.

"Done" Lorenzo tells me after a few minutes. "Barney was very good, and you can stay calm because it has no inflammation. He could only still feel a little annoyed in the next few hours, but nothing more."

"Thank you" I say sincerely, for the second time today.

"Must. However, if it happens again, don't wait too long to bring it here. Such nonsense can become a much more serious problem" he observes seriously.

"Agree. I will also tell his mistress."

Barney has calmed down, he finally stopped sneezing and starts jumping around happily throughout the studio.

Observed in this context Lorenzo really looks like a smart person, and it is immediately clear that he loves his profession very much. All in all it's not so bad.

In the waiting room I find two other people: a middle-aged woman with a German shepherd on a leash, and a boy holding a pet carrier, whom Lorenzo calls in his study.

"So, how did he go?" Ottavia ask me.

"Problem solved. Anyway is better than what he

seems like..." I say a little over-thinking.

"About who are you talking?"

"Of the vet, or better about Lorenzo" I specify.

"Lorenzo? The same guy that helped us a little while ago?"

"Precisely. And above all I was right" I say giving her a elbow.

"In which regard?" pretending to not understand.

"Why you are interested to know? You said that he is not your tipe!"

"That's right, I don't care" she say grumpy. "It only flatters me that he is interested in me, how every other woman would flatter. Except you!"

Ottavia is right. After all, she knows me too well and knows how much I hate compliments, let alone show off. We are diametrically opposed to this: Ottavia likes to be at the center of attention, in any context, and with this way of doing she has always compensated for my reserved and taciturn nature. Unlike me, she is expansive and talkative, perhaps even too often.

When we were little, although I was the eldest of the two, Ottavia always took my word for me, something I obviously could not but be grateful for.

At Christmas, for example, every year I had to recite a poem on Christmas Eve. Of course I hated that moment, which for me was a source of stress and anxiety, and I always refused to read it, not really understanding why I had to do it. Fortunately

Ottavia always came to my aid, and in the end everyone was so taken by her way of posing and talking that they almost forgot about my presence.

Looking back at those moments, I can't without a smile again today.

"Do you remember Christmas Eve? When as a child we had to recite the poetry" I ask her.

"How to forget it. For you was a real worry!"

"I don't think it would be so different now. I would still feel a terrible shame" I admit. "But you instead have never made any problem out of it."

"It's true" she admits amused. "I even recited in your place! I don't know if I did it to help you or to receive another applause."

"You were really terrible. Adorable, but terrible!"

"You did not hated me for this, right?" she asks me, seeming very afraid of my answer.

"You are kidding? How does such a thing come to mind?"

"I don't know, maybe my exuberance could sometimes annoy…"

I can't believe my sister really thinks about these things.

"Darling, listen to me: you've never done anything wrong to me, on the contrary" I say with the greatest possible sincerity, "I think I just have to thank you. And if ever I always wanted to be like you" I confide.

In a very rare momentum of affection from her

part and she embraces me.

This gesture is not from her.

Ottavia hardly expresses her feelings so openly, although her character may suggest the opposite, and perhaps it is also for this reason that she always tends to run away in love.

"I love you" she whisper in one of my ears.

"Me too little sister. You can not imagine how much" I say exchanging her hug, happy to be able to share this moment only with her.

22

Cinzia's departure is scheduled for this morning.

From today I will begin to take care of Barney full time, although with all that has happened in the last few days, the big puppy has almost gone into second place.

The thought of Sergio and of what happened the last time we met, is always present, and the moments in which I manage to drive him away are rare. The memory of his kiss continually returns to confuse my ideas, while I only wish that everything could slip away like water into a stream.

Sergio, his lips, his parfum, his breath...

Why is there no way to reset the memory?

I go out to take Barney.

While I go down the stairs I read a message that arrived:

I hope I don't have to help you again today..., it's written.

Obviously is Lorenzo. Only him could write me such as sentence. Evidently Cinzia gave him my phone number due to her imminent departure.

His words immediately put me in a good mood.

Don't worry, I don't think there will be a need, I reply, even adding a smiley face.

Lorenzo, in his way, is a nice guy and above all competent in his job, and I always appreciate those who put effort and passion in everything he does.

When I arrive at Cinzia's house, it is a relief to note Sergio's absence.

Today was the last day that I could risk meeting him, since in the coming weeks there will be no reason for me to come here.

This reflection reassures me, but at the same time it leaves me a little bitter in my mouth.

Am I really so sure I can't see it all this time?

"Agree" Cinzia tells before to great me, "I think I told you everything. Anyway, whatever you need, you can call me at the number I gave you, although unfortunately I won't always be available."

"Don't worry. Barney and I will do very well together. Isn't it real big puppy?"

"I am sure."

"I assure you that is in good hands. I will treat him as if it were mine."

"I do not doubt it, and that is why I entrust him to you. As for the rest, I'm waiting for your news. I look forward to seeing your project."

"I'll start working on it right away, and you'll see that you'll be thrilled with the result."

The only fixed point in my life is the awareness of knowing how to do my job in an excellent way. At least on this point, I never had any doubt.

"Can I ask you a question?" she then tells Cinzia.

"Tell me."

"Did something happen between you and my brother?"

"Absolutely not!" I esclaims, perhaps with excessive enhasis. "Why you ask me?"

I hope Sergio did not tell her about the kiss.

"Nothing, just a feeling..."

"Then have a good trip" I say cutting short.

"Ah, I forgot an important thing. I spoke with the owner of the appartment a few days ago, and he expressed his intention to make some changes. So I gave him your number."

"Fantastic! Thank you very much!" I happily exclaimed.

"Nothing you are welcome" she says with a wink.

"I leave you my keys, so you can come here whenever you want. I have already notified Sergio too."

This is much exciting news than the previous one, but I still have to make the best of it. I have no other choice.

Cinzia's taxi has just arrived to take her to the airport.

"Can you think of closing everything please?", she asks me greating me one last time.

"Sure", I answer.

Then she loads her suitcases in the elevator and leaves, leaving me alone with Barney. I decide to take the opportunity to take another look at the apartment.

"Well big puppy, it seems that we will give a nice freshen up to this house."

Regardless of me and my intentions regarding what will soon become only the old apartment of his mistress, Barney crouches on the living room carpet, while I start looking around with a critical eye.

The first thing I take note of in my mind, and which I had already noticed, is that the open kitchen and the living room are the absolute priorities. Cinzia's bedroom, on the other hand, is quite spacious, and illuminated by a French window overlooking a small terracee. I get closer and I open them in order to let some fresh air come in.

Outside there is only a glimpse of the sun that looks shy in the clouds, but strangely I don't care, because I still feel full of vitality.

I close the window and head towards the guest room, which obviously is now occupied by Sergio.

The walls are white, and this is without doubt the first thing I would change. The decor is simple, quite minimal, with a single bed, a small two-door wardrobe and a bedside table. I am tempted to open them to look inside them, but I do not want to do it. It would be a violation of his privacy, and I certainly have no intention of staining this crime!

However, I cannot resist the urge to sit on his bed and stroke the badsheets.

The pillow gives off his smell, I can perceive it even from a distance. Instinctively I take it in my hands, hold it to me and smell his perfume, inhaling deeply. I close my eyes and it seems to me that Sergio is next to me, and for a moment I really wish he was.

I am always so boringly sentimental that I hate myself!

I continue to hold the pillow tight while I take my cell phone out of my jeans pocket.

I start the random selection of the songs and turn up the volume.

"...Your kisses lift me higher
Like the sweet song of a choir

*You light my morning sky
With burning love...",* I sing with all the breath I have in my body, moving to the rhythm of music and letting myself go, without thinking that at this moment I shouldn't be here, holding in my hands dreams that do not belong to me...

I keep twirling around myself, until I notice that someone is watching me, and I startle when I realize that obviously it can't be anyone else but Sergio.

How long will he be there looking at me, leaning against the door frame?

"Sergio" I can barely pronounce his name with shortness of breath, given both by the effort to dance and by the surprise. Then I turn off the music and almost throw his pillow on the bed. "I was just taking a look..." I try to justify myself.

He anyway carries on staring at me.

"Don't worry" he tells me amused. "Do like as I am not here."

"I come back in another moment" I answer visibly upset. "I am sorry..."

"That you saw me like that", I would add.

Without any doubt he will think that I am crazy!

"I don't mind it at all" Sergio admits. "It's the most fun and sensual thing I've ever seen."

Sensual? Funny for sure!

He obviously making fun of me.

But why does he keep looking at me like that?

"But you are not very in tune, I am sorry to have to confess it" he admits laughing.

That smile makes me crazy!

"Now I have to really go. I bring Barney with me" I say, without being able to look at him in his face.

"Don't go, please" he whispers, almost imploring. "Why do you always run away from me?"

He can not ask me that!

I have to do, and right away.

"I am not running away" slurred, remaining on the defensive.

"It seems to me exactly the opposite" he continues. "But don't worry, I have no intention of taking advantage of you solo just because you are in my bedroom, and I just saw you singing and squirming like a real rock star!"

Damn!

But what the hell did I think of? I should have imagined he could have come home at any time.

"I came back in the coming days" I tell him, as if it were a warning not to be foun. "I believe that Cinzia has already mentioned something about this apartment."

It confirms me with a simple hint of the head.

I want to leave this room, but he is still ahead of the door and obstructs the passage.

"I'd like to go out, please…", my request appears more like a plea.

"And if I didn't want to let you go?" he asks me

getting even closer.

"I can scream" I reply, as if I want to tease him.

"I don't think you would do it."

"Don't taste me."

"You are putting me a taste..." he says close to my lips.

This is really too much!

Sergio is playing dirty. He knows very well that in this way I could even give in to his flattery.

"I think I already told you that I was busy" I repeat.

"I know, and honestly I don't care. I can not stay away from you" and he was saying this eliminating thos few centimeters that was still separating us. "Therefore now you have to forgive me if now I do this..."

I don't have time to stop it or avoid it. Sergio is already kissing me, and the only thing I want right now is to reciprocate him, as if I had never kissed anyone before. As if he were my only wish ever really expressed...

His right hand is stroking me along the back, while the other, resting on my neck, presses hard to keep me from moving back.

I feel the warmth of his tongue creeping between my lips, overcoming my resistance. The touch of his fingers is light on my skin, like a caress, and this is enough to make me excited and let me imagine already naked in his arms.

But this thought so bold causes me immediately disturbance, and I involuntarily stiffen.

"You don't have to be ashame of me", his voice is once again a whisper. "I think I lost my mind the first time I saw you, with the clothes all soaked. You were beautiful..."

What he is saying?

All this can not be real!

Probably I fell asleep on his bed, and now I am simply dreaming.

"You should not have" is the only thing I was able to say. The fear of suffering again, and of not being able to manage the consequences of yet another disappointment, they won't let me go, even if I want it more than anything else.

"If I hadn't forgotten important documents this morning, I wouldn't have come back, and I wouldn't have met you. I believe this is a sign..."

"There is no sign!" I esclaim almost screaming. "Apart from that of your obvious inattention" I say ironically, trying to ease my tension. "You have to leave me in peace Sergio. Please."

"I don't think I can do it" insists, looking straight into my eyes. "You too have felt my own emotions a moment ago. I feel it, and you can't deny it."

In a fraction of a second he cancels the distance that had just recreated between us, and I feel like his prey again.

At this point it is clear that he has no intention of making me leave, and perhaps it would be better to give up and stop fighting the inevitable.

And if he was right, and all was part of our destiny? Even the fact that I didn't marry Giulio?

All the suffering suffered as a result of it would suddenly take on a meaning, and probably one day I could even thank him. Or even more angry with him!

Surely if I got married I would not meet Sergio again on my journey. Or yes?

If it were true that everything we do in life, in one way or another, always leads us on the same path, whether we want it or not?

"I can't deny being attracted by you" I recognize in the end, even if I should stop being always so stupidly sincere.

My worst enemy is always and only me.

"You feel "attract" by me Rebecca? Really, only this?" In his eyes I read a compelling request. "I think you are scared and also quite confused, and believe me, I understand it. But you can't deny that there is something between us that goes far beyond mere physical attraction. You cannot deny to be aware of it."

He is putting me with my shoulders on the wall, and I'm feeling hunted down.

"Sergio, please. I can not manage this situation right now. I need to understand a few thing before…", I try to keep vague, as much as I can, hoping he takes a step back.

"It is your boyfriend?"

I mention a poor yes.

"You know what I think Rebecca?" he rethorically ask. "I think if you were really in love, you wouldn't be here talking to me now, and you wouldn't have any reason to be confused. At this point I believe you already have the answer you are looking for."

"But how you dare?" I scream, as if I really should feel hurt by his words, even though I am the one to blame.

Sergio seems struck by my reaction and my excessive attack of anger. "Take the time you need to clear your mind. I'll wait. I can't give you up now that I've found you."

How can I resist him if he keeps talking to me like this? Which woman would succeed in my place?

Maybe I should just let myself go. And I'm almost ready to do it, but my cell phone starts ringing.

"Sorry. I have to pick up" I justify myself, glad that someone, whoever it may be, has intervened to get rid of this very inconvenient situation.

I look at the display. It's Lorenzo.

It doesn't matter why he's calling, the only thing that interests me is to have any excuse to get out of this mess!

Sergio leaves the room to allow me to speak freely, perhaps imagining that he may be my boyfriend.

"Hello?" I answer.

"Ciao Rebecca" the voice tells me at the other end of the phone. "I hope I haven't disturbed you."

"Absolutely not", and I would also like to tell him how grateful I was at this moment.

"I'm calling you from the emergency room" he continues.

Emergency room?

"What happened?" I ask worried.

"Nothing serious. I just had a little accident with the motorbike..."

"What do you mean "a little accident"?", now I'm seriously alarmed.

"I fell to avoid investing a cat that cut me off, so I banged my head. Fortunately, however, I was wearing a helmet."

"Have you endangered your life, even risking to cause an accident, to avoid a cat?" almost the instinctive reproach.

"It seems obvious to me."

"Well, I would have done exactly the same thing" I admit. "Anyway, are you okay?", from his voice it wouldn't seem so serious.

"From a first diagnosis it would seem there is no trauma. But I still have to undergo a tac and stay for a few hours under observation."

"I understand", even if what escapes me is why he called me.

"I need a favor" he tells me.

"Ask me too."

"Would you mind coming to me to recover at the hospital?"

Why does he ask me for it? Don't you have a friend, a brother, a relative or something?

But of course I owe it to him, and being able to reciprocate what he did both for me and for Barney seems to me the least I can do. And then in this way I would also have a valid excuse to escape Sergio's attention.

"Okay" I reply. "Arrive immediately."

"Thank you. But don't rush, there is no need. I still have to stay here a few hours."

"It doesn't matter, I prefer to come immediately anyway."

I close the conversation and join Sergio in the living room.

"Any problem?" he inform.

"A friend has had an accident. Fortunately it is not serious, but I still have to go to him."

"I'm sorry..." says to be courteous.

"See you Sergio", I greet him giving him a hasty kiss on the cheek and run away, taking Barney with me, before I can reconsider or he won't let me go.

23

I get in the car. I drive quickly home, where I leave Barney, and immediately run to the hospital.

Although Lorenzo seemed calm to me, I am still worried and I want to make sure he is really well.

I park the car and go to the emergency room to ask for information. From here I am sent to the diagnostic department, where Lorenzo is already performing a tac.

I don't like being in this place. Hospitals give me some anxiety after my father had a heart attack a few years ago.

The mere thought of what my family and I spent in that period manages to transmit me a deep anguish, even after a very long time.

I sit down and wait for Lorenzo to finish the exam.

After a few minutes I see him already arriving accompanied by a nurse.

"How are you?" I ask him right away going toward him.

"Like one who has just fallen off a motorbike" he answer me in an ironic way.

"Your sense of humor is still intact. You'll get away with it!" I joke back. Now I feel reassured.

"I am sorry to have bothered you, but I have been living in Pavia recently and I hardly know anyone yet" he justify himself.

"A part from me!" I make a point.

"A part from you…"

"Anyway no disturb. And then I had to repay you, right? At least we're even now."

"Perhaps then I would have preferred you to remain indebted to me."

"And for which reason, if I should know?", although I believe I have already guessed the reason.

"Because I would have had an excuse to extort a date with Ottavia, of course."

I would have bet on it!

"If I had imagined your real intentions, I would have abandoned you here!"

"I don't think you would have done it."

"And what makes you think so?"

"Because I'm nice, attractive and terribly sexy. It would have been a waste to let me rot in this hospital, don't you think?"

"You are really bad!"

"Not so much, admit it."

"Well maybe, at the bottom at the bottom…" I say smiling. "But with Ottavia I don't think you can have much hope."

"How can you be so sure? You could be pleasantly surprised by my innumerable resources."

"I have no doubt!", and I am seriously convinced. "So should I convince my sister to accept your invitation?"

"Exactly what I meant."

"But if you believe so much in this "potential" of yours, you shouldn't need my help" precise, just to prick him a little.

"Let's say that I prefer to have an alternative plan". Then he lies down on the couch and closes his eyes. "I have a terrible headache" he says.

"I can imagine it."

While he can't see me, I look at him carefully, perhaps for the first time.

He has a slight hint of tawny beard on his face, which gives him an almost hard appearance, and his hair is all disheveled. Instinctively I would like to pass my hand through the thick hair, but I refrain from doing so. Although it is not the kind of man I would normally be attracted to, I have to admit that it is not bad at all, and maybe I wouldn't mind helping him win my sister. They would be a nice couple, very well matched, and then I like Lorenzo, despite my initial judgment. Beyond the simple physical attraction, I believe that a character like his can hold her own.

He suddenly opens his eyes and looks at me.

"You didn't resist I know. No one can do it" he says with conviction.

"But do you want to stop it? You are too sure of yourself!"

"It is true, I am. But I don't think it's bad, or isn't it?"

"No, it is not. And I think I would like to have even a bit of this security of yours."

"What a strange situation you don't think so?" he asks me.

"Yes" I answer. "And tell me, where did you live before you moved here?" I ask curiously.

At first he seems almost to need to reflect on his answer, and his distracted air makes me smile.

"I studied in Milan, and after my internship I worked for a couple of years in a veterinary clinic in the suburbs" he says. "Then a month ago I had the opportunity to come to Pavia, and here I am! But actually I come from the south.”

“I had guessed from your accent, as well as from your innate spigliazza” I confess.

“Here I have no one”, continues Lorenzo. “And always remaining closed in the clinic, I have not yet had the opportunity to make new acquaintances. Except you.”

“I’m really flattered to be your only friend then” chirping with a honeyed tone, even though I really like to consider myself that.

“Well, I’m carrying forward, since you will soon become my sister-in-law.”

“Hey, go easy boy!” I warn him. “After all, you hardly know Ottavia. You saw her only once, and for a few minutes. Is it possible that you are already so enamored of her?”

“It’s called "love at first sight" beauty! Never heard of it?”

Love at first sight.

That’s exactly what I felt for Sergio, a lifetime ago...

24

Today is my first day of high school.

I'm excited, and tonight I couldn't sleep. The changes scare me a lot, and I always live all the new experiences with an excessive dose of apprehension.

I have been in the auditorium for over half an hour.

The new members, of which I am also a member, have all been summoned here, where the professors will shortly give the usual routine communications.

I took a seat on the stands, a little apart from the others, and I eagerly wait for the meeting to begin, while students are still entering from one of the entrance doors.

Among all those faces, a smile among others attracts my attention.

I remember reading once, somewhere, that only twelve muscles are used to smile. Only twelve!

I don't know for what absurd reason, but I would like to approach that boy and be able to say to him: "Hello! I think I've never seen anything more beautiful than your smile in my life. And I just fell in love with you!"

This is probably the mysterious love at first sight that everyone talks about: butterflies in the stomach, the beating of the heart that accelerates the mad, salivation reduced to zero. I had never experienced anything like this before, and it is an indescribable feeling.

The marvelous vision, owner of the equally splendid smile, goes beyond me, and without in the least paying attention to my presence, goes to sit on the opposite side to mine.

Unconsciously, he brightened my day, and I think he made everything else around him bright. Even the math teacher, who until a moment before had seemed to me more than a hundred years old, now seems to me younger and with fewer wrinkles!

I don't know who this boy is, nor do I know his

name; I only know that what I am feeling right now is love, the one with a capital. I'm sure. And I'm so excited, I can't sit still.

I would like to go to him and have the courage to introduce myself, but obviously I stay where I am, because between my thoughts and reality there is a sea that I am not yet able to cross. So I'm happy to watch him from afar, while he chats with someone sitting next to him. Then a girl arrives. He turns to her and kisses her on the lips, in front of everyone.

I feel a CRACK coming from my chest, into which my fragile heart has just shattered.

It's amazing how events change perspective over the years.

The day I saw Sergio for the first time, I thought it would remain unattainable for me, while now I am trying to reject it.

For the duration of the assembly I had been watching him like hypnotized, and for the next five years my reaction to seeing him, every single day, would always be the same. He ignored even my name, and the very fact that he didn't recognize me is proof of how invisible I have always been to his eyes.

I had fallen in love with one look. And when love breaks into our life in this way, it escapes any control, because it is almost surreal. It's pure magic.

In my life I have read many books and theories

about love, and the one that most fascinates me, and which I consider true, is undoubtedly *the search for a soul mate.*

According to Plato, in a very ancient time, men had two heads, four arms and four legs. One day these beings tried to climb Mount Olympus to take the place of the Gods, and Jupiter to defend himself threw against them the lightning that divided the men into two parts. Since then every human being has been constantly searching for his half, precisely called "soul mate", or "another part of the apple". Our perfect half, in short, the one that completes us, making us go back to being one, the one that reflects our way of seeing life and the world.

But few are those who are lucky enough to find each other, while most are satisfied or are under the illusion of having found it, thus ceasing to seek...

25

A couple of hours have passed since I arrived at the hospital. Lorenzo and I had time to learn more about each other. Then a doctor enters the room with the results of the tac in hand.

"It's all fine" he says. "Fortunately, hematomas are not evident and he can safely return home. If you still get a headache, take an analgesic as well, okay?"

"Thank you Doctor" Lorenzo replies.

"Well, let's go!" I esclaim talking to him.

"I don't wait for anything else."

"And your motorbike?"

"I'll go and retrieve it tomorrow."

"Are you hungry?" I ask him.

"In fact, my stomac has been rumbling for a while!" he admits.

"I don't feel like leaving you alone, just out of the hospital and after some hours in the emergency room. Would you like to come to my home?" I ask without going around with words. "I prepare something to eat and I still keep you under control, then I take you home."

"I know you are attracted by my irresistible savoir faire, but you know that I have a weakness for blondes" he says with a wink. "I come only if you promise that you won't take advantage of me!"

"How stupid!" I esclaim, giving him a pad in his shoulder.

"Ahi!"

"I could seriously hurt you" I threaten him.

"I'm still in hospital. You must treat me with respect."

"If you don't stop it I immediately swear that I leave you here seriously!"

"I agree, Crudelia!" he tells me while laughing.

When we get home, I find Ottavia sitting at the

couch chatting with Andrea.

"We were waiting for you" she immediately tells me. "But where were you? I've tried calling you a lot, but nothing. And what is he doing here?" she asks looking at Lorenzo.

"Ciao little sister. You're right, I had the ringtone removed" I justify myself.

"Ciao Ottavia!" Lorenzo esclaims obviously happy to see her.

"He is the reason why I was not answering the phone" I explain.

"Ah, now is all clear" Andy whisper in an allusive tone.

"Don't start!" I reprimand him. "I only went to pick him up from the emergency room."

"Yes, but nothing to worry about" clarifies our guest, answering the implicit question printed on Andrea's face. "Anyway my name is Lorenzo" he says holding out his hand.

"I am Andrea, Rebecca's roommate" presents itself. "But what were you doing in the emergency room?"

"I had a little accident with my motobike. But I am fine."

"I am glad. And you two how do you know each other?" he question in an indiscret way.

"Then I'll tell you..." short cut. "But why did you look for me?" I ask turning to Ottavia.

"I needed to download, and I saw that you were

answering the phone...”

“When she arrived, an hour ago, she was really furious” Andy intervenies.

The image of my sister beside myself is enough to alert me. Those who know it well, like me, try to avoid making it alter.

I believe that with Lorenzo here with us tonight, we will see some really good ones!

“What’s happened?” I ask her, hoping that as usual she is the only one to magnify the facts, taken from her moment of anger.

“This is Fabio’s little one!”

“The boy I told you about a few weeks ago, remember?” She looks at me as if I were obliged to remember him.

Fabio? Honestly no. And anyway if I had to keep in mind all the names of the boys with whom my sister comes out, I would need a database!

I wonder when she’ll decide to finally put her head right.

“Refresh my memory.”

“But yes! That guy I met in the gym” she insists.

Total void.

“Are you sur eyou told me aboutg it?” I dare.

“Of course I told you about it! However it doesn’t matter” says visibly irritated. “That useless being has left me!” yells. “You understand? *HE-LEFT-ME!*”, scans the words one by one, as if to make me understand even better the meaning of what he just said.

"Indeed this is an exceptional event" I conferm. I think it never happened that a boy left her.

"Catastrophic you mean!" she continues to yell.

"Stay calm, you know as we say: *"Close one door, a big doorways opens up..."* Lorenzo mentions.

Magnificent! All we needed was his wisdom pills.

Ottavia will eat him alive!

Please don't add anything else, or you'll be done for!

Ottavia as a man has never had very clear ideas, or rather, her only conviction is that he never binds too much to anyone. It is for this reason that she continually changes partners (I do not believe that a boy next to her has ever lasted more than three or four months at the most!), without the knowledge of our mother, of course, that if only she were aware of her behavior would be completely unacceptable. I myself tend not to approve her attitudes, even if I admit to feeling a certain envy for her way of facing, without thinking too much about the future, but fully enjoying only the present. In this she and Lorenzo are very similar.

"It does not seem appropriate to make it a tragedy", I say trying to play down and soften her anger.

"How can you say it?"

Now she seems calmer, and if I didn't know her

too well, I could swear that the tone of her voice was almost cracked.

"Isn't it that you fell in love with it, and that's why you're so sick?"

"In love with Fabio I? I hope you're joking!" esclaims her almost offended.

Even if she would, she would never admit it.

"Of course he was fantastic in bed, but from here to being in love with him..." she says frankly. "And then you know that I never lose my head for men."

"Never say never! There will always be a first time in life..." Lorenzo intervenes again.

I believe that today I really decided to end his existence.

If nothing serious has been done by falling off the motorbike, apparently he has every intention of going back to the hospital with a broken limb!

"But why do you keep getting involved?" Ottavia asks, again annoyed by his intrusiveness. "This speech does not concern you. You don't even know me!"

"To this we can immediately remedy, don't you think?"

"I don't think about it at all! You're not my type!" my sister replies dryly.

"You could change your mind", Lorenzo insists.

"I don't think so!"

Oh God! Here we risk going on forever!

There is no escape with these two.

Fortunately Andrea intervenes: "Careful friend, you are playing with fire" says amused

My sister is a far too determined girl, and it's almost impossible to get her to change her mind; if you put something in your head it is immovable, and Lorenzo with his behavior is certainly not opening up a gap in the walls of her hostility.

"How about preparing dinner?" I ask, before the spirits begin to heat up further.

Now the unrepentant Casanova has a vague idea of what awaits him, and I am beginning to hope that he will not give up on his intent.

"How did you fall off the motorbike?" Ottavia asks at some point, while we are eating.

Her curiosity seems to be a positive sign.

"Avoiding a cat..." Lorenzo answers with carelessly.

With three simple words he could already have conquered her, and in fact she seems to be very impressed.

"I love cats! I would love to have one more."

"You would like to have an entire farm" I say.

"You're right. If I still didn't live with mom and dad I think I would have the house invaded by animals of all kinds!" she says biting an apple.

"See? We have already found a common point" he hastens to point out to her Lorenzo. "And who knows, maybe it's not even the only one..."

Here we go again.

"Lorenzo is Barney's veterinarian" I interrupt him by turning to Andrea. "But we met at the park a few weeks ago. The other day also helped me replace the punctured rubber."

"The right men at the right moment" Andy tells winking in the direction of Ottavia.

"He moved to Pavia recently and he does not know anyone" I continue, trying to make my tone seem as sorry as possible, in an attempt to plead his case to my sister. "But fortunately he met me..."

Throughout the rest of the evening Lorenzo did not miss an opportunity to make himself brilliant and attract the attention of Ottavia, who gradually seemed to melt with every new joke.

Regardless of the outcome that he will have in his quest to break into her heart, I am very happy for this friendship that has just blossomed. With his exuberance and spontaneity, Lorenzo managed to distract me from Sergio's thought, so much so that I no longer thought of us, nor of our kiss; but left alone, it took only a moment because the memory of what happened only a few hours ago resurfaced with arrogance, leaving me completely helpless.

How did I get myself into a similar mess?

I don't know how to get out of it, and for some strange reason I have the distinct feeling that things can't do anything but get worse.

I put myself in bed with this ugly premonition
that oppresses me, hoping that at least once I may
be wrong...

26

I'm lying on the sand on the beach, enjoying the
last rays of the afternoon sun.

I look at the horizon in front of me. The sky is
clear. There is not even a cloud to soil this perfect
blue with white; not a breath of wind to mess up my
hair. The sea is a table. Everything is still, too quiet,
and I finally feel peaceful.

I am continuing to fix a point in front of me for some minutes already. I like this immobility, and it gives me peace.

There is no one else but me. Only the cry of the seagulls keeps me company, and the slight rustling of the waves that break on the shore and then retract, dragging small pebbles and shells with them.

As a child I loved collecting them, and I was soon on the beach with my father to collect the most beautiful, while my mother and sister stayed home to sleep. He and I have always been early risers, especially on vacation, when we heard the call of the sea already at dawn.

This is why I have always loved our summer holidays in Sicily, my father's land of origin. Every summer I stayed at least a month in the house of my granparents, before starting another strenuous school and work year.

Now I'm here, watching the sun go down until it disappears behind the horizon line.

I have a mind free of all thoughts. No worries, no anxieties and insecurities, no fears. There is only me, in the company of myself, and it is a very pleasant feeling of peace.

I would remain in this paradise forever, on this beach sheltered from the rocks, but just a moment and suddenly the scenery turns into hell.

In an instant the boundary that separates the sky

from the sea disappears, and in its place appears as from nothing a wave that becomes increasingly higher as it progresses.

I remain still, terrified and fascinated at the same time. I know I should run away, or I'll be overwhelmed soon, but I can't move.

The wave is always more impetuous and closer and closer. Suddenly I recover from my state of tranche and I start to run as fast as I can. But that enormous mass of water leaves me no escape, although I try with all my strength to stay afloat, and it overwhelms me, dragging me with it, until no trace remains of me.

I open my eyes in terror.
I'm in my room and I just had a nightmare.
Another.
I have sweat on my forehead and a parched throat, as if I had been running for miles without a break.
I take a sip of water and look at the clock: it's still six in the morning.
This is the third time that I have had this dream, which also becomes more and more distressing.
The first was the week my father had a heart attack. I remember it like it was yesterday, because I felt exactly the same feeling of terror and helplessness. The second a few days before Giulio canceled our marriage.

This nightmare seems to be the mirror of my life: it reflects my insecurities and the fear of being swallowed up, of not being able to react and of being overwhelmed by events.

This time what will it mean? What ominous omen will you be about to face my horizon?

I would not let myself be influenced by a dream, even if it is so absurdly real as to leave me unsettled and powerless. However, I don't think I could ever get back to sleep. Therefore I go to the livingroom, where Barney is sleeping on top of the carpet with Honey crouched beside him, and I seat beside them.

Barncy opcns his sleepy eyes, looks at me and closes them, puffing.

How I envy him! I need an entire box of sedatives to be able to go back to sleep, so many thoughts are stirring in my head. Sergio, his kiss, his words... But above all my innumerable lies.

How can I be angry about how he treated me so many years ago, if I'm making fun of him myself? And what is worse, is that now we are no longer two boys as then. Therefore, seen in this perspective, my behavior appears to be nothing short of despicable!

I make myself a coffee.

Andrea gets up and follows me into the kitchen.

"Something threw you out of bed?" he asks me sarcastically, just to make me notice that strangely I got up before him.

I ignore him.

"Has there been an earthquake while I was sleeping?" insists.

"You are not at all witty. And if you really want to know, I still had that dream…"

"Which dream are you talking about?" he asks me. Then he reflects: "Ah yes of course, the one where you meet the man of your life and live happily ever after!"

"I wonder why I still lose time talking to you" I say nervous.

"Why are you so upset? I just wanted to play it down."

"I'm worried" I admit.

"Now there is no need to wrap your head before you are broken. You will see that it is only the fault of all the stress you have accumulated during this period."

"Let's hope so."

"You just have to stay calm. I am sure that this time nothing will happen for which it is worthwhile to fret so much."

Here, he said it!

These are the last famous words!

But I am increasingly convinced that something will happen in the coming days, and that this "something" will probably have something to do with Sergio.

Besides, my meeting with Cinzia could not be all roses and flowers, there had to be some thorn along the path!

I have breakfast quickly.

I need to clear my mind a little. So I decide to go for a run in the park and then go to the villa, hoping not to have bad surprises even today.

27

As soon as I arrive at the place, I immediately go to work. I open my notebook and begin to make some sketches on how I plan to furnish every single room: two bathrooms, three bedrooms (one of which will be used as a fitness room), a huge living room, a kitchen with a central peninsula, and a huge garden, where one could easily build a tennis court or a swimming pool semi-Olympic.

I must admit that at this moment it would be impossible not to feel a shred of envy towards Cinzia. My apartment is certainly not small, but in comparison to this house there is no comparison that can stand. And then the total independence that offers the ability to live in a context like this, without condominium meetings and quarrels with neighbors, is priceless!

But after all, my home reflects what I am, and at the moment I don't think I would change it, even if I could afford to do it. Only when Giulio left five months ago did I feel the real need for renewal, because everything made me think of our life together and what I had lost. Then luckily Andy arrived, and gradually living with him managed to heal some of my injuries.

One morning, unbeknownst to me, he showed up behind my door with his suitcases - at least ten! - and he had settled in my house. Since then I have never felt alone.

Without further delay (also given the fear of receiving unwelcome visits), I finish my drawings, recover Barney, who is still roaming the garden, and come home.

Opening the mailbox, amidst the usual flood of advertising flyers and some bills to pay, I find an envelope that immediately attracts my attention.

For Misses Rebecca Spalti, I read.

Intrigued, I open it immediately.
Inside there is an invitation.

Dear Miss Rebecca,

We are pleased to invite you to the inauguration of

"Memoire"

that will be held on the 24 October

Follow address and the time of the event.

But what does it mean? There must certainly be a mistake. Perhaps a case of homonymy.

Look inside the envelope and notice a folded white piece of paper I hadn't seen before. I don't know the calligraphy, but at the bottom of the card is there Sergio's signature.

Now is all clear!

How did I not think about it right away? The

restaurant in question is by Sergio. Here is the reason for the invitation I have in my hands.

Hi Rebecca,
I really hope you will be present for me this evening
is very important, I read on the ticket.
The invitation is also extended to a second person.
So feel free to bring with you whoever you want, even your boyfriend if you believe, so I would finally have the opportunity to meet him.
Good day.

Sergio.

This was not needed!

And now what do I invent?

Maybe a sudden departure...

No, it would not be credible because of my commitment with Barney.

A sudden illness of any kind then...

No, even worse. Surely I would pull on some other disaster!

But I could always have a planned commitment for some time, or a cold, or a migraine attack. Anything short! Any idea that won't let me go to this damn opening!

With my boyfriend then... There is no boyfriend damn me!

It is evident that Sergio is testing me. In all

218

probability he does not believe that there really is a man in my life, and he wants to understand how far I can go.

I agree then, if this is what I want I will go to his inauguration with my boyfriend, so maybe he will leave me in peace once and for all.

But the real problem is another: where do I find a man who can play the part?

Well, I could always pay someone to do it; exactly like in that American movie that I have watch at least ten times. What was it called? Now I don't remember...

Moreover the story of the protagonist, Kat, is very similar to mine. She, too, given up by her boyfriend without much explanation, is then invited to the marriage of her younger sister. But since he doesn't feel like introducing himself as a single - too humiliating as a condition - he decides to "rent" a professional escort, with the aim of making her ex jealous.

I don't think I would never be able to pay someone to play the same part, also because I would die from embarrassment. So there is no solution. The only thing to do is to invent at the last minute any excuse to decline the invitation. Besides, I'm certainly not forced to do anything against my will, even if a part of me would like to accept. Curiosity is already beginning to make its way in me, rowing against me.

Sergio had not mentioned the imminent opening of his new restaurant, and I would love to see it. Perhaps also due to a certain professional deformation, I imagine it refined and elegant.

However, I still have a few days before the event, and I have plenty of time to think about what to do. I will try to ask Andy for advice. Surely he is the only one who can help me make the right decision without making further confusion. It's a real pity that I can't let him play the part of my boyfriend (a role that would have been perfect in any case), since Sergio has already known him as my roommate.

If only there was someone else who could ask an absurd favor like this...

Then I have a lighting.

Of course! I don't understand why it didn't occur to me before.

There is another person I could ask, and it is Lorenzo.

I'm sure he won't tell me no.

We should only agree on some details about our relationship, such as where and when we met and things like this, and the game will be done! And if you really had to refuse, I could always convince him by giving him an appointment with Ottavia. She would kill me if she found out, but basically I'd do it for a just cause.

Well. Now that I've come to this conclusion, I feel much calmer.

I would like to send a message to Sergio to tell him that I will go to the inauguration, but maybe it's better not to be too impulsive and wait at least until tonight. I have to talk to Lorenzo first, so I decide to call him right away, even though I'm afraid he's working right now. In fact, his phone rings a couple of times, until the answering machine is attached.

I think it is useless to leave a message and it is better to recall it later.

This invitation story has displaced me. Moreover, I am certainly not a girl for parties, social events and things of this kind. Regardless of our personal situation, and of having to present myself with a fictitious boyfriend, I would still be uncomfortable with so many people I don't know.

As if that weren't enough, I'll also have to look for something elegant to wear, and I don't like this idea. I never wear anything that is not jeans or anyway clothes that of feminine have very little.

I already imagine Andrea's expression when I give him the

news. Surely he will be the only one to be enthusiastic about it.

It's time for lunch and I try to call back Lorenzo, the only one who can save me from this absurd situation.

"Hi Lorenzo. How are you?" I ask when he answer the phone.

"Hi little sister in law!" he esclaims.

"Ok, I would say that you are definitely better!" I say amused.

"Thanks for the interest. I know you've already grown fond of me."

"Maybe, a little bit..." I had to admit. "But actually I would have called you for another reason too", I hesitate for a moment.

"Ah, you women! You always have a second purpose..."

"Stop it! You know that I would have call you anyway."

"I know" he says sinceraly. "Come on shut! It has to do with Barney?" he asks.

"No, this time has nothing to do with Barney. But I would need a little personal favor, indeed not really small in truth..."

Now that I find myself asking him seriously, I feel a certain shame, and it's fortunate that he can't see me in the face. After all, we still know each other very little, despite the various events of the last few days.

What if he judges me wrong? Well, it doesn't matter.

The worst thing that can happen to me is that he gives me crazy and I answer no.

"Rebbi, are you there?"

"Yes, it is that I find myself quite uncomfortable in making this request to you" I confess.

"At least try" he press me.

"Here you see… I would like you to play my boyfriend for one night" I say all in one breath.

"I got it right?" he asks incredulously. "Do you want me to pretend to be your boyfriend?"

"Exactly."

"In what kind of trouble di you get Rebecca?" he asks me bluntly.

How the hell did you figure that out?

"No trouble" I lie, pretending to be almost offended by his insinuation.

"Ok, then what would be the reason for this bizarre request?"

Indeed seen from his perspective, and without a logical explanation, the request actually sounds strange. If I had been in his place I would at least burst out laughing, and I'm grateful he didn't.

"I will have to attend an important event", I start to explain, "and I wouldn't want to go there alone."

"Only this? Sure?"

His acuteness is really tiresome, but I think he deserves to know at least part of the truth.

"No, not only this" I recognize it. "In truth I put myself in an unpleasant situation."

"I thought so."

"I told the person who sent me the invitation to be sentimentally engaged, so this same person also invited my boyfriend. The problem is that in reality there is no boyfriend! All clear now?" I tell without interruptions.

"Very clear. What is not clear to me is why you chose me. I know you have a secret attraction towards me, but I only see you as a friend, you know it!" he jokes.

"But is it possible that you never take anything seriously?"

"This is why I will be perfect! The idea of playing the part of your boyfriend seems to me very funny" continues.

"I knew it. I didn't have to ask you."

I had to imagine that he would have had a good time behind me.

"I was just kidding! I will, if I can help you."

"Really?" The biggest problem is solved therefore

"Sure" he answer firmly. "But you have to take a little curiosity: why on earth would you have told this person to be engaged?"

His question is completely legitimate, but I don't want to give him too many explanations.

"It is a long story. Maybe I'll tell you another time..." I remain vague.

"I like amorous intrigues!" he exclaims.

"Just to clarify: there is no love intrigue."

"If you say so... But I don't see any other reason why a girl should invent a non-existent love story, if not for a very specific reason, namely to make another man jealous."

"You're wrong!" I reply categorically. "It's not like you think."

Or maybe yes?

"You know that if I help you, you will once again be indebted to me?"

"Don't worry, I know perfectly well how to repay me."

I'll think about how to tell Ottavia later. Better to take one step at a time. "We still have a few days to define some details. We will have to try to be credible and study the part well, I would not like Sergio to suspect something" I say without realizing it

"And so it is Sergio the name of the mysterious man that you would like to deceive."

Of course, putting these words in my ears sounds bad to my ears too.

"It is not a real deception" I say trying to justify myself. "Rather it is a slight alteration of reality."

"Slight alteration?" repeats Lorenzo. "Tell me in what absurd reality you and I could ever be seriously engaged?"

Long live sincerity!

"It would be so terrible to be engaged to me?"

"That was not what I meant" he tries to correct himself immediately. "You know well that I find you a beautiful girl, but you also know that I am interested in your sister, therefore I don't believe that there is any possibility that between me and you there can be nothing else, if not a splendid friendship."

"Thank you for making the situation so clear."

"Welcome. But as you can see you can't talk about "slight alteration"."

But who do you think you are, maybe my conscience? I begin to regret asking him for such a delicate thing. Not to mention that in reality he is perfectly right: mine is a beautiful and good lie, like all those I have told so far of the rest.

What a bad person I am becoming! But now I think it's too late to go back and feel remorse. I have decided: I will introduce Lorenzo as my boyfriend, Sergio will put his soul in peace and maybe he will stop to give me the torment!

"It would be the case to see each other in these days" I take word again changing the topic.

"I'm coming to dinner tonight?", he immediately catches the ball.

The intrusiveness and the impudence of this boy still leave me puzzled, although I am learning to know him better.

It was not difficult to convince him to play my game, but the idea of going out with someone other than Giulio, even if it is only a fiction, seems to me increasingly unlikely. I just hope I don't end up a victim of my own deception.

Thanks for your kind invitation.
Lorenzo and I will not fail.
See you soon.
Rebecca.

I press the enter key without second thoughts.
Now the die is cast.

28

"Now can you explain me?" Lorenzo asks me as soon as he enters my house.

"There is not much to say…"

Please don't insist!

"If we are to be complicit in this staging, I think it is better that I know as much as possible about it."

"All right" I say at the end, although I am still very reticent about talking to him about it. "This is the inauguration of a new restaurant. The owner is Sergio…", I stop for a moment.

"Go ahead" he spurs me.

"This person and I attended the same high school" I begin to tell. "At the time I was in love with it, but I always remained in the shadows. After school, for ten years we never saw each other again until, very recently, we met by chance."

"However, the reason for your lie remains unclear to me."

"Wait, I haven't told you everything yet" I'll take it back. "Barney's mistress is Sergio's twin sister. This is why we met again, even though he didn't recognize me."

So I end up telling him about my various adolescent vicissitudes, until Lorenzo interrupts me. "All clear now, and I understand very well."

"Seriously?"

"Right. I also had some problems during my school years. Let's say I was the favorite target of the various bullies on duty. At the time I was the exact opposite of how you see me now."

"I don't believe it!" I exclaim. "I don't see you at all in the guise of the helpless victim!"

"Instead it is so. And now that you've told me how things are, I'm even more convinced that I want to help you."

I was so worried for no reason.

"And then" he carries on, "I'm really curious to see what Sergio will do when he sees you kissing a handsome boy like me!"

"Wait a minute, who said that we will have to kiss?"

"Well, if we want to be credible in his eyes, we'll have to do it, don't you think? Don't worry, I'll sacrifice myself with pleasure."

"But listen to this a bit presumptuous!" I tell, threwing him the pillow of the sofa.

"Hey! Is this the way to treat your new boyfriend?" he asks, feigning offense. "In fact, I would say to start doing some technical tests immediately."

"Stop it now or I'll look for a new partner, and goodbye appointment with my sister!"

"See that I say it only for you" assures me. "A couple that does not exchange effusions in public is boring and not very credible."

"I really think we will run this risk then!"

Left alone, I begin to review the plan that I agreed with Lorenzo.

We will pretend we met last year on vacation. Perhaps it will seem a bit banal, but certainly very likely.

After having frequented each other during our stay at the beach, we had lost sight of each other for a few months, until last winter he had moved to Pavia for work reasons and... BUM! The spark struck again between us.

A simple love story, like many others, without too many useless frills.

After all, I don't think it will be so difficult to play the part, I just have to be able to look very, very in love. For Lorenzo then it will surely be a walk. He is casual, spontaneous and self-confident, a real wasted talent!

It was undoubtedly a perfect choice; not that I had many alternatives regarding the rest.

There are only a few days left until the inauguration, and I know for certain that my agitation in the meantime will continue to increase to an incredible extent, but the only thing that matters to me is that Sergio believes in our farce.

This time I am determined, and I have no intention of retracing my steps. Keeping him away from me is the only way not to allow myself to fall in love with him again, even though I'm probably making one of the biggest mistakes of my life.

Of course Andy will not approve my behavior, but I am the only one responsible for my choices, and I will not allow anyone, not even him, to interfere or make me change my mind. I will go all the way, whatever the cost.

29

I look forward to end this day as soon as possible, and it's only seven in the morning.

I'm so thrilled that I can't stay in bed a minute longer. So I get up, have breakfast and go for a run to break the tension

Cinzia yesterday proved to be particularly enthusiastic about the sketches I sent her, and we discussed them at length, until the conversation inevitably moved to the opening of the new restaurant.

"Sergio told me that tomorrow you will be also there…" she had mentioned.

"Yes, I'll be there."

"You didn't tell me you were engaged" she added.

"On certain subjects I tend to be a bit reserved", I justified.

"Really a pity. I was hoping that something could be born between you and Sergio" confesses without turning round.

This was obvious!

"I don't think it will be possible. I'm happy with Lorenzo", I lied.

"I'm happy for you, but a little less for my brother. I think he cares a lot about you."

That sentence had been like a slap in the face, and left me undecided about the possibility of continuing my initial purpose.

Throughout the night I continued to reflect, so much so that I could not fall asleep except at dawn. But since I opened my eyes this morning, I can't help but wonder if I'm doing the right thing.

Damn! I can't afford to have second thoughts right now.

Somehow I would like to be able to free myself from this weight that does not allow me to breathe and to reason clearly, but I cannot. The certainties that I had until yesterday, today have turned into boulders, and weigh on me now more than ever.

I come home to change and go to Michi.

When I leave his salon a little later, I already feel like another.

The hairstyle is absolutely perfect in its simplicity. I only hope to resist until tonight, which I hope I can do too.

Now I just have to find a dress that makes me look nice and elegant, so I enter hopefully in the first store; but unfortunately I don't find anything to do with my case, and in the meantime I have already lost more than half an hour to try on different clothes. Short to the knee, long with side slit, narrow shoulder strap, strapless, decolleté, high-necked... There is not even one that makes me look like I would like to see myself.

Thank goodness it is just an evening, because I could not bear all this stress for a long time!

In the second store the situation does not improve at all. I still lose time, and now almost on the brink of despair I enter the third, already completely discouraged.

At the entrance I immediately get received by a shop assistant.

"Good Morning", greets me with a beautiful radiant smile.

What will it have to smile so much? Blessed is she who has a reason to do it!

"Goodday" I answer, trying to be equally kind, despite my bad mood.

"If she needs help, I'm at her disposal" she says affably.

"Thanks", I say just as lively, just so as not to appear rude.

I begin to look around, but after a few minutes I realize that nothing seems to do for me.

Now yes I start to worry!

Will it not be that I cannot find even a dress that is suitable for me, because in my subconscious I am not at all convinced of wanting to go to this inauguration?

I'm about to turn on my heels and leave, but the shop assistant of a moment ago is approaching again. "Can I help you?" she asks me with the same tone as before. "Are you looking for something in particular?”

“No, but thank you anyway”, I free myself up instantly firmly. The girl immediately loses her sparkling smile and walks away, wishing me a good day.

Maybe I was a little rude, but right now I’m so nervous and frustrated that I really don’t care a damn!

I can’t take it anymore for shops.

All this is not for me!

Perhaps in my closet I will be able to find something that can adapt to the circumstance. I will certainly have at least one dress bought for a particular occasion and never worn again. And luckily for me in the last few years I have not gained even a kilo!

It’s six o’clock in the afternoon and I only have a couple of hours left to get ready. But since I don’t know how to dress yet, I begin to fear that they won’t be enough.

First of all I decide to give myself a nice regenerating bath, exactly what I need to relax my nerves, which are now tense like the strings of a violin.

While I wait for the tub to finish filling up, Andrea returns home.

“What are you doing here already?”

“I came to save you!”

"What do you mean?" I ask him, already anticipating his answer, at the very moment when I realize that in his hand he has a couple of bags from a well-known clothing brand.

"What did you think about wearing for this evening?"

"Well, here..." mumbling. "I tried to buy something that was suitable, but..." I try to exonerate myself, like a girl just caught red-handed while she discards a candy she's just been forbidden to eat.

"But?" he urges.

"You know how I'm made! I got nervous, and finally decided that I would recover something from my wardrobe."

"From your wardrobe?" he asks me, almost horrified. "I knew it! You are incorrigible!" he exclaims raising his eyes to the sky. "Come on, try these. The size will certainly be the right one", he says, handing me the bags.

"But, Andy..." I do to reply.

"Don't argue and try them. Immediately!"

I wonder why he should always be so authoritarian.

"I agree", I know very well that it would be useless to protest.

"Come on, hurry up. I don't think you have much time left."

He's absolutely right. And then I still have to

wear makeup, which is not really my forte.

I then open the first bag and take out a little black dress.

Thing? No mention of it at all!

Andrea knows very well that I would never wear a dress like this. It's really amazing, but it's nothing short of skimpy!

"I think I would feel uncomfortable all night with this dress on" I try to oppose it, hoping to be able to dissuade him from his goal.

"I really don't understand you Reb" he insists. "There are girls who would make false papers to be in your place, and have your body. You instead continue to devalue yourself, always dressing yourself in a way that to define a little feminine is just a kindness."

Why should I change what I am for this stupid reception? I don't find it right!

"After all, how important will be how I dress this evening?" I ask, raising my tone a little too much. "I would like to remind you that I must not impress Sergio, on the contrary, the exact opposite! This is the only reason why I decided to accept his invitation, to which I will introduce myself with a fake boyfriend by my side!" I conclude all in one breath.

"Rebbi calm down now" says Andy more calmly. "Regardless of what your intentions towards Sergio are, I won't let you make a fool of yourself." Then he grabs me by the shoulders looking into my eyes. "You will be splendid this evening, whether you like it or not! And you won't get out of here except with that dress on. Is it clear?"

We also missed Andrea.

I have no other choice, unless I don't want to risk leaving home for real! I know he would be able to.

I go to my room with Andy in my wake. I take off my clothes and put on the sheath dress, which he is immediately ready to tie behind my back. I also put the heel twelve pumps that he bought for me, and I'm ready to look at myself in the mirror.

"Wow!" he exclaims. "You are absolutely breathtaking. I knew I wasn't wrong."

"It is beautiful Andy, really" I have to admit while I continue to mirror myself, almost making it hard to recognize myself in the image I see reflected.

The dress wraps me to perfection, leaving my shoulders uncovered and, alas, even a good part of my legs. It is sober and fine, with a lace appliqué on the front.

"This is your blank canvas" says Andrea, helping me to put the cover on my shoulders. "Now we will complete it with some accessories and the right makeup."

"You are aware of the fact that I will never be able to walk on these stilts right?" I complain.

"But Lorenzo will be there to support you. What are you worried about?"

"I will do the figure of the clinker!"

"You are perfect instead, and if only you had a bit of self-esteem you would be even more so."

I know how much his words are telling the truth, but obviously the term *self-esteem* has never been part of my vocabulary.

"Thanks Andy. You saved me again" I say hugging him. He hugs me tightly, transmitting all his strength and affection to me.

Suddenly, however, I remember having left the tap of the water open in the bathtub, therefore I run to the bathroom, where the water was about to leak out of the bathtub.

I undress once again and immerse myself in the steaming water, stretching out every single muscle.

The next step is put on makeup, and since I've never been a lover of lipsticks and flashy colors, I opt for something very light: a little black eyeliner and a veil of eye shadow; mascara, nude foundation, a touch of blush and lip gloss to complete the makeup

I revive my hair, which with the fatigues of the afternoon have weakened slightly; I put a few drops of perfume, a pair of drop-shaped earrings with glitter and a necklace that makes pendant, and I am finally ready.

"You are simply charming" confirms Andrea once again admiring me.

"Thanks" I say smug and equally embarrassed.

If even my best friend's compliments make me uncomfortable, how will I sustain the gaze of others? Not to mention Sergio's.

The intercom is ringing. My knight tonight has just arrived.

I take the dust coat and the clutch bag, also this a present from Andrea, I greet him and close the door behind me.

As I feared, balancing on these vertiginous heels turns out to be an undertaking right from the start, and after a few steps I already have serious difficulties in standing. But now I can't do anything about it. I certainly can't go back and change. Andrea would kill me at least!

While I wait for the lift I think of what Lorenzo will look like, and I just can't imagine him dressed formally. Instead I leave the door and seeing him I am pleasantly surprised.

He wears a light gray suit, white shirt and even a tie. I never would have said it, but he is really very attractive dressed like that, and he seems to be at ease too, unlike me.

As a true gentleman he comes towards me and hands me his arm. "Mademoiselle, you are absolutely divine this evening."

"You also are not bad at all" I admit, handing him the car keys, and trying not to stagger too much in the few steps that separate us from my car.

Lorenzo opens the door for me, then sits in the driver's seat and starts the engine.

"So, are you ready to face this evening, *my love*?" he asks me, putting particular emphasis on the last two words.

"Not at all, *my darling*" and I burst out laughing, which seems more hysterical than amused.

"Trust me. We are a perfect couple!"

I believe I have never been so upset, not even at my first appointment with Giulio, yet even that time my tension could have been cut with a knife so it was palpable.

30

Giulio and I made an appointment for ten o'clock. I am very agitated and I am no longer in the skin.

My aunt Anna and my cousin Sara seem to be tense even more than me, since this is the first time I go out with a boy. So much so that they could hardly believe it when I gave them the news.

"It was time for you to decide to put your nose out of the house!", was the first thing Sara had said.

"I don't think it's an obligation to go out with someone" I reiterated a little annoyed, as she continued to torment me.

I'm ready to go out, but I'm standing in front of the bathroom mirror for more than ten minutes.

"It is better that you give yourself a move" shouts Sara outside the door. "It's half past nine and you still have to wear make-up."

Still with this story?

"I have no intention of wearing makeup. I've already told you!" I shout back.

I never liked putting all that stuff on my face.

Unlike my cousin, who never leaves home (not even to go to university), if she doesn't have at least a pencil line on her eyes.

"Don't say idiocy Reb. Of course you have to do your makeup!" replies imperative.

"Sara, leave her alone" reproaches her mother. "Even if she is right" she says then turning to me.

"Aunt! Do you put yourself in it now?" I ask, exasperated. "Thank you very much to both of us, but so I feel more at ease!"

"You are happy" Sara says with a false tone of surrender.

I think I'm finally ready, but my stomach is in turmoil.

I dressed in light jeans and a turquoise shirt, my favorite color; flat shoes and hair tied in a braid.

"Of course, looking at you, you wouldn't say that you're going on a date with a boy" Sara grumbles with disappointment. "If tomorrow you won't want to know about you anymore, then don't come and tell me that I didn't warn you!"

"Don't worry, it won't happen. And anyway in the case I believe I would continue to live anyway", so saying I take the bag and leave the house.

"I can't believe it!" I hear while I close the door. "She didn't even wear heels!"

I smile to myself.

She and I are so different... Her character looks a lot more like that of my sister, and maybe that's why I'm so fond of her.

I asked Giulio not to come and get me at the house. I prefer to take a walk on my own to have time to metabolize what for me is still a completely new situation.

Our appointment is at the entrance of the pub *La Rosa Nera*.

I am perfectly on time and also Giulio, who is already waiting for me at the entrance.

Now I can't go back any more, even if along the way I have often thought of doing it.

When he sees me coming, he comes towards me, greeting me with a kiss on the cheek, then together we enter the room. I have never been there before, since I am not a girl with a particularly active social life, but it is very nice and there is a nice atmosphere, even if I continue to feel uncomfortable, and I fear that he may notice.

"Do you feel like drinking something?" he asks. "Here they serve excellent drinks."

"Ok" I only answer. Take a look at the list and order a non-alcoholic drink.

"Is the same also for me" Giulio says to my surprise.

We begin to talk about the preparation of our respective exams, and gradually my tension melts away. Giulio is a nice and very bright guy; he can amuse me and make me feel inevitably attracted to him.

We talk nonstop for more than two hours, also discovering that we have several points in common, and at the end of the evening he offers to take me home.

As we walk next to each other he takes my hand, and this unexpectedly inexplicable contact gives me confidence, a bit like we have known each other for some time.

Then suddenly he stops, brings his face close to mine and tries to kiss me.

I am taken aback. I don't know if I have to and above all if I want to return his kiss, and I become elusive.

Now for sure he'll think I'm just a stupid girl!

Instead Giulio lifts my chin, forcing me to raise my head and look into his eyes.

"Stay calm" whispering softly touching my lips, "I will not try to kiss until you will be asking me."

We continue to walk in silence, once again hand in hand, to the door of my house.

"Thanks for the wonderful evening" I say awkward.

"I just hope it wasn't the first and only time you gave me the honor to go out with you."

His voice is sweet and persuasive. I look into his eyes and see them sincere, clear and clean. Then I don't even think about it for a moment, I get close and place my lips on his.

Giulio seems almost surprised by my sudden and unexpected audacity, but he returns my kiss without hesitation. His lips are warm and taste good, and I really didn't think it would be so nice to kiss someone.

It is a spontaneous and primordial instinct, a chemical attraction that pushes us towards another person and that we cannot in any way oppose.

We remain tight for a long time in each other's arms, staring at each other dreamily, as if simply by taking our eyes off the magic of the moment can vanish.

I wish I was not so clumsy!

But in the end I decided, I put aside all my stupid fear and we exchanged a long and tender kiss.

My first kiss...

I AM IN ECSTASY!

I think it was worth the long wait. He is so kind as to seem almost like a boy of other times, and I can't wait to see him again tomorrow, and in the coming days again...

31

The drive takes only a few minutes.

Sergio's new restaurant is not far away, but obviously with these heels I could not do more than two steps on foot.

I'm really very curious.

Furnishing a restaurant is no small task. It takes a lot of skills, and absolutely no kind of improvisation, especially if the venue in question will have to welcome an elegant and refined clientele. The furnishings and other accessory elements, as well as the atmosphere that one intends to give, the space available and the type of the place itself, must best reflect the chosen style. We must study in detail how to distribute the surfaces, the arrangement of the light points, and enhance, where possible, the architecture and the surrounding landscape. Finding the right design, choosing colors, decorating walls can often be really complicated.

In short, it is not a simple undertaking. I myself had had quite a few difficulties when I was given this task for the first time. But following my instinct I managed to get the desired result, making the owners of the place very satisfied.

If there is one thing I learned from my work, and that I try to always keep in mind, it's that when you put effort into anything you do, the results come sooner or later, even if at times it may seem the opposite. And exactly as it happens in everyday life, there is never an ideal solution for everything and everyone, and this concept in my trade is always and in every case true.

After parking the car, Lorenzo once again hands me his arm to help me get off.

Despite being more and more upset, I feel reassured by his presence, and I still have to try to maintain a certain demeanor, if I don't want to risk making a terrible figure in front of everyone. Unfortunately I am not used to worldliness, in fact I would say that my social life is closer to that of a cloistered nun, especially since I broke up with my ex. Normally he managed to drag me out of the house at least on Saturday night, although most of the time I preferred to stay on my comfortable sofa watching a movie on TV, and Giulio often satisfied me. But all too often in recent times he happened to come out with his friends, leaving me alone, and the rest could certainly not claim that he too isolates because of me.

Looking back now, with a clear head, all this should perhaps have made me understand how much we were really very different from one another.

Many argue that character differences serve to enrich the couple. I think instead that sometimes, when these are too many, or too obvious, although the feeling is strong, there is nothing that can be done to keep it together. As has happened to us.

Perhaps if I had tried to change even some of the aspects of my character, things could have gone differently. Or not. Who can say?

But would Giulio have been willing to change for me?

Probably my need to have a person next to me, and not feel alone, was so strong as to make me put aside our incompatibilities.

Giulio was impulsive and always acting instinctively. He could tell me "I love you" even dozens of times a day, but I don't know how much those words were really heard, and not simply dictated by habit, even though I never doubted his feelings towards me.

For my part, I have always seen the world in pink. Emotional to the point of crying even before the romantic scene of a cartoon, perhaps precisely for this reason I tend to prefer gestures to words, especially the simple ones of everyday life. A hug, a ticket left on the bedside table to say good morning in the morning, or breakfast served in bed. All those little attentions that warm the heart, filling the days and life itself.

There are already many people in front of the restaurant.

"I can do it! I can do it! I can do it!", I continue to repeat to myself.

"Be sincere" I say turning to Lorenzo. "How do you see me?"

"You really are very beautiful Rebecca, seriously. And if I hadn't lost my head for your sister, I could also have tried it with you tonight" he says holding me tight more than necessary. "So be careful not to let me drink too much!" he says allusively.

"It is you who must be careful, especially where you put your hands, *darling*", I reply with a half smile.

"Don't worry. You know I am a true gentleman."

"It will be better for you, and for your beloved family jewels!"

"Damn, I didn't make you so violent!"

"You don't know me well enough yet, *my love*."

It continues to seem so strange to use these nicknames with a person who is still almost a stranger to me. But this too, later everything is part of the game.

We enter the restaurant and are immediately greeted by what I presume to be the maître de sala.

"Good evening. You are the gentlemen...?"

"Good evening" I answer him. "I'm Rebecca, Rebecca Spalti. And he is Lorenzo, my boyfriend."

The man takes a quick look at the list in his hands and makes us sit down.

"Take a seat" tells us. "Give me your coat madame" he adds, turning to me.

In this precise moment I perceive that this will be one of the worst nights of my life!

I feel completely out of place, because of this place, my dress and a fake boyfriend by my side, and I wonder for what absurd reason I decided to accept Sergio's invitation.

Perhaps this would be the most opportune moment to turn around and leave.

Besides, he still doesn't know I'm here, and I could always call him tomorrow, inventing some plausible excuse for my failure to attend tonight.

"I think it would be better if we leave" I whisper in the ear of Lorenzo. "I don't feel like going on..." But I don't have time to finish the sentence, because I am interrupted by Sergio's voice.

"Ciao Rebecca", he greats me.

Too late.

Let the staging begin!

I turn to him.

"Hello", I say with a tone of voice so calm that I can even amaze myself.

"I'm glad you managed to come."

Known, with a touch of complacency, that is looking at me from head to toe with undisguised admiration. He says nothing, but from his look I perceive that I will have to thank Andrea for the dress he forced me to wear.

Sergio is impeccably dressed, as befits the occasion (although I would have loved to see him wearing a chef's outfit), and it is nothing short of perfect. But on the other hand, even wearing a poor rag would have exactly the same effect on me. And then he has always had an athletic physique, and I am sure that over the years he can only be improved.

More than once in high school it happened to see him bare-chested in the men's locker room at the gym. The boys almost always left the door ajar, so it was inevitable not to see anything.

The first time I saw him, in passing, I was completely dazed.

"What is it Spalti? I bet you've never seen a naked boy in your life!" one of his friends had laughed at me.

I immediately became purple, and ran to lock myself in the bathroom. I was ashamed to die, and I was afraid that I would never be able to look at him again after that episode.

Now, on the contrary, it is he who looks at me almost confused, and it is strange to realize once again how in life the roles can be reversed in a completely unexpected way.

"This is Lorenzo, my boyfriend."
That's it, I said it!
Now I can almost breathe a sigh of relief.
"Very pleased" they both say shaking hands.
Sergio almost seems to want to challenge him to a duel, and I would pay to know what's on his mind right now.
"Excuse me a second" he says then, moving away to meet a woman who is coming towards us.
"Carola, how nice to see you", he greets her by kissing her hand.
"I would not have missed this event for no reason" exclaims the latter.
Tall, elegant, in her forties and with a good bearing, she immediately gave me a feeling of jealousy.
I have no idea who this person is, but I don't like the way she is looking at him, with that very confidential manner.
"Who is that beautiful lady?" Lorenzo asks me.
"I have no idea" I reply annoyed. I don't like seeing him near another woman, whoever she is.
"You are very tense, even more than before. You almost look like a rope about to break."

"Stop making comments!" I say altered.

"As you are susceptible, *darling.*"

His words make me smile and manage to dampen my tension. Moreover, taken by anxiety, I have not yet had the opportunity to observe the restaurant carefully, even if from a first and very quick look, I recognize being sought after as I imagined it. But it may be that the agitation always gives me a certain appetite, the first thing that strikes me are the round covered tables with immaculate tablecloths and overflowing with food!

I'm already looking forward to being able to throw myself headlong into the buffet to appease my atavistic hunger.

"I'm getting a certain peckish" Lorenzo confesses, guessing my thoughts. "It would be a real shame not to take advantage of it. Do you feel like it if you get something?"

"Well, since we are here..."

Lorenzo walks away towards the tables, leaving me for a single moment. Maybe it would have been better to go with him, but I no longer have time to follow him.

"And so are you Rebecca?" the same woman asks me a moment ago.

How do you know my name?

"Yes, my name is Rebecca" I answer. "But I don't think I have the pleasure of meeting you."

"I am Carola, a family friend. I've known Sergio

since he was a child."

A family friend.

Now I feel like a perfect idiot for thinking who knows what!

"Very happy" I say a little embarrassed.

"Now it all seems clear..." she continues looking at me carefully and giving me a wide smile.

"Excuse me?" I don't understand what she is referring to, but I immediately notice that her attention is no longer addressed to me.

"Erica. What are you doing here?" she asks the girl who has just approached her.

"Hello aunt! Aren't you happy to see me?" she breaks in.

"Sure..." replies Carola with little conviction. "She is my niece Erica" says turning to me again.

"Sergio's girlfriend", specifies the latest arrival.

What? It is not possible!

Even Carola seems to be amazed by the news.

This would be the opportunist harpy!

Why did Sergio so insistently make me come here tonight? I do not understand. To humiliate me perhaps, it seems obvious to me. And I was going to fall for it!

"Rebecca, *darling,* are you okay?" Lorenzo is asking me, just back loaded with food from his tour at the buffet tables.

"Yes, I'm fine" I reply, trying to recover from my state of shock. "I just got to know Erica, Sergio's girlfriend, and her aunt Carola" I explain doing the presentations, and placing particular emphasis on the word *fiancée*.

Lorenzo looks at me confused, but fortunately avoids asking questions, while I can't help but notice that Erica's face is full of pleasure.

I observe her better and I realize, to my great satisfaction, that without all that makeup to cover her face, it would not even be this great beauty.

His features are too strong, almost masculine, and I wonder what Sergio could have found in this girl. I don't see her at all next to him, and I definitely don't like her at vibe, regardless of the fact that she has just revealed to me that she's the girlfriend of the man I'm in love with.

Finally I managed to confess it to myself: I'm in love with Sergio!

I came here, bringing with me a person who has been pretending to be my boyfriend for an hour, and all this to convince Sergio to get away from me. Instead I find myself being the victim of my game. I set up this little theater for nothing. But how could I have been so naive as to be fooled by his words and his way of doing?

"I don't feel very well" I whisper to the ear of Lorenzo. "I think it would be better to go..."

I don't want to stay here a minute longer. This farse lasted too long.

32

I retrieved my coat and I am almost at the front door of the restaurant.

The only thing I want right now is to get my nose out of here as soon as possible. But Sergio's voice keeps me again.

"Are you already going away?" He asks from behind me.

"Yes, I'm sorry. A strong migraine broke out" I answer, turning around, trying to justify myself with a very trivial pretext, while I just want him to let me go.

Behind him I notice the figure of a slender and distinguished boy.

"I'm very sorry" says my interlocutor. "But at

least let me introduce you to Alessio, my business partner and longtime friend."

Alessio? This name is not new to me, as is the person to whom it belongs, and it is enough for me to reflect a fraction of a second to be able to remember and put the elements together. He was a classmate of mine, and a friend of Sergio's in high school.

All this is absurd!

For sure I'm just dreaming. In a moment I will reopen my eyes and all this will remain only one of my many nightmares.

"Wake-up Rebecca. Wake-up!", I scream to myself, but unfortunately nothing happens. I'm still in this place, with two pairs of eyes on me.

Then it's all true.

This guy is really my former schoolmate, and if he recognize me it would be a disaster!

I have no way out. My only hope is that he, just like Sergio, no longer remembers me.

I suddenly realize that Alessio is telling me something, I hear his voice, but my brain refuses to metabolize his words.

"Rebecca... I am sure I know you" he states without the slightest hesitation.

Anything that could remove me from this circumstance, at this moment would be welcome. Even the collapse of the entire restaurant!

"I don't believe…", I say, keeping my head down trying to escape his inquiring gaze, and shamelessly denying the evidence, hoping it will work with him too.

"For sure! You are Rebecca Spalti!" he says even more convince. "We were in class together in high school, don't you remember?" insists.

"Absolutely not" I still deny it with all my strength, even though it is now clear that I can no longer escape the inevitable.

"You changed" he continues, "in better, if you permit me. But I am sure I am not wrong. Your eyes are always the same."

"Do you know her?" Sergio intervenes.

"Of course yes! But don't tell me you don't remember her?"

"I don't know what you're talking about."

"She is Rebecca! She attended our high school. She was my classmate."

During their brief discussion of my identity, I continue to remain silent. There is nothing I can say, and perhaps it is better this way, because I could do nothing but worsen an already decidedly catastrophic situation.

Sergio, for his part, seems to be making an enormous effort so that *this Rebecca* can re-emerge from his past, while I would simply like to shrink and PUF!, burst like a soap bubble.

Also Lorenzo continues to stare at us, without

however deciding to intervene. Even he was speechless in the face of the ugly turn of events.

I think it's time to throw the mask. It no longer makes sense to carry on this comedy, and it is only up to me to give the necessary explanations.

"You are right" I admit to break the ice, turning to Alessio. "I'm just what you believe. It's nice to see you again after all these years" I say trying not to make the voice tremble too much.

"Then is true?" Sergio asks me.

"Yes" I answer guilty.

"Now I understand why I had always the feeling to know you!" exclaims, as he looks at me as if he were seeing me for the first time and didn't know exactly who I am.

"Sergio, I...". I wish I could explain to him how things are, but the words die in my throat.

"Ten years have passed, but I could not have failed to recognize you" Alessio interrupts us. "I had a crush on you in high school" he confesses without embarrassment. "Even if you have never had eyes that for the beautiful and tenebrous!"

All this does not make sense.

Sergio has just discovered the truth about me, and from his expression I can't understand what's on his mind right now; while Alessio confessed to me that he had been in love with me in high school!

Other than the plot of a film, reality is definitely more convoluted!

"Why did you pretend not to know me all this time?" Sergio asks me.

"I'm sorry. I didn't want to lie to you."

"You would not have wanted to, but it does not seem to me that you have had so many scruples. You've been teasing me for weeks!" says blatantly altered. "For what reason? Was it a trick you used to make me pay?"

So he remembers everything!

"Is not like you think..." I try again to justify myself.

Lorenzo please do something! I implore him with my glance.

Fortunately, he understands and pulls his cell phone out of his pocket.

"Darling, I just got a very urgent message. A patient of mine is sick. We have to go."

Oscar-winning acting!

Any other excuse, however, would have been welcome.

"I'm sorry, Sergio. You have to believe me" I say in the most sincere tone I can find.

"I don't think I can do it", and so saying he turns and starts to walk away. But an instant later he looks back and retraces his steps. "And no! I won't let you go like that. You owe me explanations, not find?" he ask almost threatening.

"She really don't owe you anything!" Lorenzo intervenes in my defense, in a tone that may have been too bright.

Some guests are looking at us visibly curious, and among them I can't help but notice the face of Erica, on which is printed an unmistakable smile of victory.

My companion girds my waist with his arm, taking me outside, and I let myself go completely to his support.

I want to go home, take this dress off, throw myself in my bed and sleep for a whole day, or maybe even two!

As I leave his restaurant, I still feel Sergio's eyes on me.

Did I want to get rid of him? I succeeded perfectly! And only now I realize that maybe this wasn't really what I wanted.

"Everything all right?" Lorenzo ascertains as soon as we get into the car.

"I don't know" I say sighing. "I ruined everything."

"So it would seem."

"You are not very helpful in this way."

"As they say: "Who is the cause of his illness...""

"Ok, I understood perfectly! It matters little now" I say resigned. "Maybe this is how it had to go..."

"The circumstances in life go in the direction in which we decide that they go", it contradicts me.

"You're wrong. I believe that we cannot escape destiny" I reply. "It was destiny that I had to meet

Sergio again on my way, like this as it was written that tonight there was also Alessio at the inauguration, and all the rest...”

“It can also be” it gives me reason. “But it was you who decided to invent all those lies. Destiny has nothing to do with it. Much of our life depends only on our decisions, right or wrong that they are.”

“I lacked your philosophical spirit!” I say smiling. “Anyway thanks. If it hadn’t been you, I don’t know what other tragic aspect the evening would have had.”

“I am convinced that you would have known how to manage it very well even by yourself.”

“I wouldn’t be so sure. For a moment my brain went completely in tilt.”

“In fact it was a really unpleasant moment.”

“Don’t turn the knife in the wound, please!”

Lorenzo takes me back home, then gets on his motorbike and darts away.

Left alone, I inevitably think back to what happened this evening, to Sergio’s words and to his accusing eyes, and in a certain sense I think I should be grateful to Alessio, because even if in a brusque way, he took an enormous weight off me.

“Are you already back?” asks Andrea when he sees me coming home. “Has something happened?”

My face speaks by itself.

“You can not even imagine”, I answer threwing

myself on the sofa' and taking away the damn
twelve heel shoes.

Long last! I couldn't take it anymore. I don't know
if the worst torture was to keep them at the feet or
to face the evening just passed.

Then without neglecting any detail I begin to tell
everything.

"Damn, not even in the best soap!" exclaims
Andrea at the end. "Did I really lose all this?"

"It wasn't funny at all!"

"Wasn't that what you wanted?" he asks,
returning serious. "You put yourself in this
situation."

"You talk exactly as Lorenzo" I say frustrated. "I
know, I did one stupid thing behind the other. I
thought that removing Sergio from me was the right
thing, but now I realize that I was only afraid of
falling in love again."

"I am sorry" he try to console me. "But you must
not despair. To all these is a remedy."

"Not this time."

"Don't be so tragic" he scolds me. "First you
should call hhim tomorrow, without spending too
much time."

"And you really are convinced that after all the
lies I told him, he still wants to hear my voice?"

"You will never know if you don't try."

"Yes, but you're leaving out a fundamental detail:

Sergio has returned with his ex" I refresch his memory. "Basically he also plaied with me. Therefore I would say that at this point we are equal."

Andrea remains silent for a few moments, then looks at me and asks me: "But he wasn't him who told, right? This is an important detail" he analyzes.

Actually no, it wasn't him. So?

"Whether it was Sergio or not, the result does not change."

"Maybe you're right, but if I were you I wouldn't trust that Erica much."

"What do you mean?"

"That could even have lied."

Andy's hypothesis is not completely meaningless, but then how do you explain your presence at the restaurant? And then why should she do it?

I don't understand anything anymore!

A very bad headache broke out, this time seriously. I have to go to bed, try to sleep and above all not to think of anything. Tomorrow I'll probably see things in another light and I will have time to make the necessary reflections, but now I really don't have the strength.

"I'll make you an herbal tea" says Andrea.

"Thanks, but first help me to loose this dress."

I go to my room, put on my pajamas and get under the covers. After a few minutes Andy arrives with a steaming cup in his hand.

"Drink it, you will see that you will feel much better."

I have never liked herbal teas, while for Andrea they seem to be the right remedy for any physical or psychological illness. In any case, I indulge him, and drink the boiling liquid in small sips, immediately feeling his heat sink down to my stomach. Then I place my head on the pillow and close my eyes, but my cell phone begins to vibrate, signaling the arrival of a message.

And if it was Sergio?

Fearful I pick up the phone and with relief I realize that it is Lorenzo.

His concern for me arouses tenderness, and after all I think he can be right: our destiny can also be written in broad terms somewhere but in life there is always free will, and in the end we are always the only one who decides which way to go.

Seen from this point of view, everything immediately acquires another meaning, especially my innumerable mistakes...

33

Two long weeks have passed since the opening night. Since then Sergio and I have not heard each other. I didn't find the courage to call him, and I certainly can't blame him for not doing it.

A few days ago Cinzia called me.

"I haven't hear of him for a while..." I had answered vaguely when she asked me about her brother.

"He does not answer to my calls" she confessed

me very worried. "He wrote me just a short messagge. But I know him well: if he doesn't feel like talking to me, something must have happened."

Initially I didn't know whether to tell her the truth and in the end, after several delays, I had told her everything, even about Erica.

"You're definitely mistaken Rebbi" Cinzia had said, flying over the rest of the story as if it didn't matter. "Sergio would never go back with that girl."

"Instead it's just like that. It was her who told me." I had confirmed, thinking again of that triumphant smile of her.

"It's all the work of her twisted mind, I'm sure."

Even Andrea had said the same thing.

"But why should she have come up with such a lie?"

"I don't know this, but Erica would be willing to do anything to get back with Sergio."

"But it was at the party. How do you explain this?"

"She will surely have found a way to convince my brother to be invited, but I assure you that between them there is nothing left" she said with conviction.

"It doesn't matter anyway…"

By now I ruined everything, so that there is still Erica in his life or not, I would no longer have the courage to be part of it.

"Sure it matters" she had reiterated, "Sergio has feelings for you."

This sentence continues to wander in my head and there is no way I can erase it.

How could I have been so blind and superficial?

Sergio has really changed during all these years, the only one that has still remained the girl of the past is just me. I closed myself towards the whole world, I isolated myself, feeling unsuitable and not accepted, and I never allowed anyone to get closer to me than I should. And this new awareness I owe above all to Alessio.

Having discovered that he was in love with me even when I considered myself just an *ugly duckling*, opened my eyes. It's a bit like when you try to focus on a distant point, but you can't do it because you are too far apart. Then just take a few steps closer and everything appears immediately clear and linear.

Similarly, if I had changed my point of observation, I would have realized all this a very long time ago. But unfortunately it is often not easy to believe in oneself and bring down those veils that mask insecurities and fragility.

From all these thoughts came the idea of creating my own blog. A sort of online diary that aims to help other girls not to make some typical mistakes (those I made myself) that are committed in love and in relationships with other people.

I think, having reached this point, I have now become aware that happiness must be sought, pursued, grasped and held tight with all our strength, without waiting for her to find us.

Everything I experienced during my high school years and in my relationship with Giulio, up to ruining the feeling that was born between me and Sergio, I think is enough to give me the faculty to transmit these new certainties of mine, (achieved through a tiring and full of obstacles) to others.

It will be true that my love life is a total failure, but when it comes to that of others, everything suddenly becomes simpler, so much so that - and in this I was inspired by Lorenzo - you can even infuse wisdom pills, which may seem like discounted concepts, but which in reality are not at all.

1- NEVER, and I emphasize never, FEAR NOT TO BE AT THE HEIGHT of someone or something.

2- NEVER FEAR EXPRESS YOUR OWN FEELINGS, or that these are not returned.

3- ALWAYS BELIEVE and anyway IN YOURSELF and on your possibilities.

4- FOLLOW THE HAPPINESS EVERY MOMENT, without worrying about the risks that could be run.

5- Better to live a life of remorse than to have a single and only regret.

I decided to call the blog *"followwhatmakesyouhappy"*, because that's exactly what I'm going to do from now on.

I write every day, just like it was my diary of the past, telling episodes related to my love life and more. I describe my total inexperience with the other sex, my being awkward in any situation, my complete lack of self-esteem and femininity, and so on.

Unexpectedly I started to be very followed, and to receive comments asking me for more specific and personal advice, so much so that I'm almost evaluating the idea of changing profession and becoming a consultant!

It is very rewarding to help others get better with themselves, even through a few simple suggestions.

The girls who write to me generally are young, but more and more often it happens that even more mature women want to question themselves, telling their experiences. And certainly the possibility of not having to talk to each other, does not generate in them the fear of being judged, making them sure to express themselves in total freedom.

This is precisely the reason why I also started writing...

Epilogue

Cinzia returned to Pavia this morning.

I'm really happy to see you again, even if that means separating me from Barney.

The time in his company has flown, and certainly from today I will feel a little more alone, since I have become accustomed to his presence, and Andrea hardly ever returns home, more and more often staying at Marco's.

But there is another reason that torments me, and not a little, and it is the possibility of seeing Sergio again.

It has been weeks since the opening night, and throughout this time I have often thought of writing a letter to explain the reasons for my behavior, but in the end I always gave up doing it. His refusal would be yet another stab that I could not bear, even if sooner or later I will have to decide to take the first step...

"A life of remorse is better than one and only regret."

Besides, Andrea has always been right. He had warned me from the beginning, and I never wanted to listen to him. I am stubborn, perhaps too much, and this aspect of my character has not always turned out to be positive, placing me as the gods limits that I often failed to overcome.

Here's another thing I will no doubt have to remember to write in my blog:

6- Listen to the opinion and advice of the people who are close to us, who care about us and our happiness.

But this is just the beginning for me.
A new beginning...

"It's a life I dream of loving you"

by Cristina Tata

Author Cristina Tata

Translated by Daniela Anedda

All rights reserved to the author.